AND THE GEN

Francis Henry Durbridge wa   ...n, Yorkshire,
1 1912 and was educated at Bradford Grammar School.
e was encouraged at an early age to write by his English
cher and went on to read English at Birmingham
iversity. At the age of twenty one he sold a play to
e BBC and continued to write following his graduation
hilst working as a stockbroker's clerk.

In 1938, he created the character Paul Temple, a crime
ovelist and detective. Many others followed and they
ere largely successful until the last of the series was
ompleted in 1968. In 1969, the Paul Temple series was
apted for television and four of the adventures prior
this, had been adapted for cinema, albeit with less
ccess than radio and TV. Francis Durbridge also wrote
the stage and continued doing so up until 1991,
en *Sweet Revenge* was completed. Additionally, he
ote over twenty other well received novels, most of
ich were on the general subject of crime. The last,
al *Encounter*, was published after his death in 1998.

Also in this series

FRANCIS DURBRIDGE

Paul Temple and the Geneva Mystery

COLLINS
CRIME
CLUB

COLLINS CRIME CLUB

An imprint of HarperCollins*Publishers*
1 London Bridge Street
London SE1 9GF
www.harpercollins.co.uk

This paperback edition 2015

First published in Great Britain by
Hodder & Stoughton 1971

Copyright © Francis Durbridge 1971

Francis Durbridge has asserted his right under the Copyright,
Designs and Patents Act, 1988 to be identified as the author of this work

A catalogue record for this book is
available from the British Library

ISBN 978-0-00-812572-1

Set in Sabon by Born Group using Atomik ePublisher from Easypress

Printed and bound in Great Britain

MIX
Paper from
responsible sources
FSC

Chapter One

Paul Temple had returned to the real world after ten long
weeks of concentration on death, disruption and deduction.
He found to his relief that the world was not at war, he
wasn't being sued for libel and his wife was still radiantly
attractive. All good reasons for a celebration.

'Darling, how nice,' Steve murmured as they went into
L'Hachoire, 'I haven't been here before.'

'They do the best pigs' trotters in London,' said Paul.
'They were recommended to me by my publisher.'

'Ah, Scott Reed. Was he pleased with the new novel?'

It was one of those exclusive little restaurants that achieve
rustic simplicity at conspicuous expense, with genuine décor
and furnishings from Provence and genuine Provençal chefs
and waiters. There was a lot of unvarnished wood, an oven
range squandered space that could have been occupied by
three tables and a dog replaced three possible diners. The
place was crowded with rather trendy Londoners and a few
slightly surprised French tourists. The head waiter showed
them to a table in the corner marked 'Reserved'.

'No no, we haven't booked –' Paul began.

'A cancellation, Mr Temple. Please be seated. Madam.'

The pigs' trotters were called *pieds de porc Sainte Menehould* on the menu, and Paul felt obliged to order them. The wine waiter brought the sherries they asked for at once and later produced a 1953 vintage Burgundy which they hadn't asked for. Paul hoped that Steve wouldn't notice the celebrity treatment they were receiving. It would have made her suspicious.

'You didn't answer my question, darling,' she said. 'Did Scott rub his hands together with joy at the book?'

'He hasn't read it yet, but I suppose he'll call it a classic story of its kind. He always does.'

'You sound jaded.' Steve laughed mischievously. 'When you finish a novel you always become like a woman who has just made love, rather tired and slightly depressed. The only remedy is to begin again or take a holiday. Darling, that's a good idea – why don't we take a holiday?'

Paul raised an eyebrow in mock surprise. 'Do you feel depressed after –?'

'It's a dangerous mood. You're inclined to become involved in other people's crimes or contemplate writing a heavyweight psychological study of murder. Let's go away while you still have your mind on me.'

'Yes, why not?' He paused thoughtfully and then said, 'How would you like to go to Switzerland?'

'Gstaad?'

'Gstaad, or Geneva, wherever you like.'

'I'll think about it.' Steve quickly refilled their glasses. 'Yes! I've thought about it. But if we go to Switzerland –'

Paul finished the sentence for her. 'You'll need an awful lot of new clothes, darling.'

'Well,' Steve laughed, 'it's true, isn't it? You wouldn't want me to look twelve months out of date.'

'A fate worse than death,' Paul agreed. But he knew as he spoke that he was being tiresomely male in joking about her clothes. 'I want you always to look as elegant as you do tonight,' he added gallantly.

They discussed Switzerland for the next half hour. Steve wanted to book a hotel and arrange a flight immediately and Paul was reluctant to go before Friday. He was being interviewed on Friday by a lady from one of the posh Sunday papers, and Paul didn't want to postpone it. She was bound to talk about symbolism in his work and the place of good and evil in the English detective novel. She would produce the kind of article that pleased Scott Reed.

'Scott still feels that if a novel is popular he shouldn't have published it,' Paul laughed. 'But a piece of pretentious criticism will knock ten thousand off my sales and he'll be able to tell his accounts department that it's literature.'

He would have developed the idea, but Steve's attention had strayed to a bland man at the table by the service door. He was wearing a well cut grey suit and made-to-measure shoes. The carnation in his buttonhole added a single touch of flamboyance.

'Paul, that man over there keeps staring at us.'

'I thought,' he said flippantly, 'that elegant women were accustomed to approving stares.'

'Do you know who he is?'

Paul nodded. 'I've seen his photograph in the business supplements. He's a financier called Maurice Lonsdale. He owns a lot of property in the West End, including several restaurants. As a matter of fact, I think he owns this place.'

'How disappointing. I thought the man who owned this would wear a beret and have a perpetual Gauloise hanging from his lip.'

The financier took a cigar from his waistcoat pocket, summoned the head waiter for a brief consultation and then left through the service door. It had been a minor intrusion, and Steve was quickly back on the subject of ski trousers.

'Mr Temple?' It was the head waiter. 'Excuse me, but Mr Lonsdale wonders whether you could spare him a few moments, when you have finished your meal. Perhaps I could take you to his office . . .'

Paul glanced across at his wife and shrugged. 'I always enjoy meeting millionaires, don't you? They help to reconcile me to being merely well off.'

'What does he want?' Steve asked severely. 'Paul, I'm not having anyone come between you and my holiday in Gstaad. Just be careful!'

Maurice Lonsdale was not the traditional unhappy, ascetic millionaire; his office at the top of the building was luxurious and smelled of cigar smoke. He poured them large brandies and waved to the antique sofa and armchairs.

'Please sit down, Mrs Temple. Mr Temple. I'm grateful to you for coming. I hope you'll forgive me for staring at you just now, but when I saw you sitting at that table I could hardly believe my eyes.'

'It's a first class restaurant, Mr Lonsdale,' said Steve. 'No need to be surprised –'

'It seemed such a remarkable coincidence,' said Lonsdale. 'I was talking to Scott Reed only yesterday about you, and I was meaning to give you a call.'

Paul sank back in the deep armchair and warmed the brandy glass in his cupped hands. He avoided the sharp glance from Steve. 'What were you going to call me about, Mr Lonsdale?'

The man hesitated apologetically and sat behind the old oak desk. 'It may sound fanciful, Mr Temple. I expect I'll be wasting your time.' In spite of the good taste in dress, the grooming and good manners, Maurice Lonsdale had an edge of ruthlessness that was difficult to pinpoint. Perhaps it showed in the voice, with its trace of a Manchester accent, or in the watchful eyes. He was feigning the apologetic manner.

'I wanted to discuss my sister Margaret. You may remember her as Margaret Beverley, she was an actress until six years ago when she married Carl Milbourne.'

'Yes, I remember her,' said Paul. 'Although I didn't know she married Carl Milbourne. He was killed in a car accident a fortnight ago.'

'Yes, he was killed,' said Lonsdale. 'But of course, you probably knew Carl. I suppose as a novelist you know most of the publishers in London.'

Paul was about to agree that he'd met Carl Milbourne once or twice at literary parties when Steve intervened. 'Where did his accident happen?' she asked suspiciously.

'In Geneva.'

Paul looked suitably astonished at the coincidence, but she merely glared at him.

'It was a dreadful business,' Lonsdale continued. 'Margaret, poor darling, has been in a terrible state since it happened. I can tell you, Mrs Temple, the last two weeks have been pure hell for her.'

'It must have been a dreadful shock,' Steve said reluctantly. 'Was she with her husband when it happened?'

'No, he was in Switzerland alone, on business. One afternoon he went for a walk and was knocked down crossing the road. I had to take Margaret out to Geneva to identify the body.' He emptied his brandy glass and shuddered. 'Believe me, that was quite an ordeal. The body was difficult to identify. Carl was appallingly smashed up, his head had been crushed –'

'It must have been an ordeal for both of you,' Paul cut in.

He nodded. 'Poor Margaret was always highly strung, but I'm afraid this has quite unbalanced her. That's why I wanted to discuss the case with you, Temple. You see, she's got this extraordinary idea into her head that – well, that Carl isn't dead.'

'Isn't dead?' Paul repeated in surprise. 'But surely you were satisfied? You saw the body?'

'Yes, I saw it.' Lonsdale poured them all more brandy. 'The body was mutilated, but it was Carl all right. I'm positive it was Carl.' He returned the bottle to the tray and remained there, fidgeting with the array of drinks. 'Apart from anything else, I recognised the suit he was wearing. Carl had absolutely no dress sense. Nobody else would wear a mustard coloured suit like that.'

Then why,' asked Steve, 'should your sister think it wasn't her husband who was killed?'

Lonsdale sighed and went back to his desk. 'Well, for one thing she consulted a medium. A very well known medium, I believe, among people who know their mediums well. Margaret asked her to get in touch with Carl and the medium failed. Failed completely. I'm afraid Margaret thinks this proves that Carl is still alive. It's ridiculous, of course, but you know what women are when they get ideas into their heads.'

It was logical, Paul thought, although not very sensible.

'To make matters worse for Margaret, she seems to have quarrelled with Carl just before he left for Geneva. They normally got on well together, but on this one occasion when they did happen to quarrel . . .'

It was an unpleasant irony, Paul agreed.

'I'm afraid my sister's completely dominated by this obsession of hers,' Maurice Lonsdale was saying. 'So much so that she's made up her mind to consult you, Mr Temple.'

Which was the second time that Lonsdale had made an equation between mental imbalance and talking to Paul Temple. Paul decided he had reservations about the successful businessman's sensitivity. 'Why should she want to consult me?' he asked.

'Can't you guess?' Lonsdale was supercilious. 'She wants you to find her husband for her.'

Paul rose to his feet. He thanked the man for the warning and for the excellent brandy. It was time to continue the evening.

'I hope you'll be nice to Margaret,' Lonsdale said. 'Listen to her, listen to all she has to say.' He opened the door and held out his hand. 'But please, for her sake, don't take her seriously. The poor darling isn't herself these days.'

Steve shook his hand and smiled icily. 'It's not really surprising, is it, Mr Lonsdale? You know what we women are like – we sometimes take things very much to heart.' She swept from the room leaving Lonsdale staring.

Paul followed her down to the street in silence. It was a full moon and the Thames was looking serene, the reflections of light almost motionless in the water. He took Steve's arm and went along the Embankment in search of the car. They passed Cleopatra's needle before he ventured to speak.

'I love Westminster in January –'

'I'm not talking to you!'

'Oh.'

They walked past the spot where Paul had thought the Rolls should be. It wasn't there. He remembered that he had parked by a pillar box. Perhaps it had been another pillar box.

'The whole evening was set up,' said Steve. 'You knew about that publisher and his mysterious accident. Scott Reed arranged the meeting with Lonsdale and I was taken for a prize idiot!'

7

Paul stopped and held on to her hand. 'Hang on, darling, that isn't quite true. Scott isn't as clever as that, and incidentally we seem to have lost the car.'

'Well, I'll tell you one thing: I've lost interest in going to Geneva. I want a holiday in the Highlands of Scotland.'

'All right,' said Paul as he glanced up and down the road, 'we'll go to the Highlands of Scotland.'

'And I hated that man –'

'So I noticed.'

Steve launched into a savagely accurate imitation of Lonsdale's manner. 'You know what women are when they get ideas into their heads,' she said angrily. 'Of course I know what women are! Paul, are you listening?'

'Yes, darling. But I'm afraid the car has vanished.'

'Serves you right.' She chuckled unsympathetically. 'I hope the newspapers make an idiot of you in the morning. Paul Temple's Rolls Stolen, that's what the headlines will read, Private Eye Sends for Scotland Yard.' The thought seemed to cheer her up and she took his arm again. 'I'm sorry, darling,' she said softly. 'It's very worrying. What are we going to do?'

They walked across the road to Scotland Yard.

The M1 was beautifully clear before them like a yellow band stretched forward into infinity. There were a few long-distance lorries on their way to Edinburgh flashing private signals at each other, an occasional car, but Den Roberts cruised smoothly past them all. It had always been his ambition to steal a Rolls.

'Goes like a bird,' he murmured for the fifth time.

'Yes,' said Lucas. 'Listen, keep it down to seventy. We don't want the law to stop us.'

He was cautious. Den had wanted to drive through the gates of Buckingham Palace and watch the sentries salute. They could have driven round the parade ground and out again, nobody would have stopped a Rolls. But Lucas wanted to reach Birmingham by midnight.

'I still think we should have hoisted an ordinary car,' Lucas grumbled. 'I mean, a mini can be re-sprayed and sold for a few hundred quid. But a bloody Rolls! You suffer from delusions of grandeur!'

Den grinned happily. He didn't try to explain. Lucas was a petty thief and he would die knocking off the occasional mini between stretches inside. But Den was an artist, he had soul. Through two years of Borstal he had sustained himself with the knowledge that he would drive his own Rolls one day and have every copper on point duty salute him.

'You don't need to worry about the number of miles on the clock with a Rolls,' said Den. 'You don't need to worry about what year it was built. This is British craftsmanship!'

'Shut up. We're being followed.'

Den peered into the driving mirror at the glaring head-lamps behind them. It was impossible to see the car and it dazzled his eyes just to look. 'Shall we leave it behind?' he asked. 'We could easy –'

'I don't know. Maybe it's trying to overtake us.'

'Yes, maybe,' Den muttered. 'Although it's been on our tail for a few miles now.'

It was worrying. The other alternative was to stop. And if it were a police car. . . The car behind them slowed down as well. Den sighed and prepared himself for battle.

'They're coming round on us,' Lucas hissed. 'Quick, do something, Den, for God's sake. Let them stop and then try a racing start to leave whoever it is behind.'

Den glanced over his shoulder as the car drew level with them. It was a large black saloon – a Rover, probably, although it was too dark to be certain. He couldn't quite distinguish the people inside it, though there seemed to be two, and the second was crouched by the open passenger window. Pointing a revolver at Den's head.

'My God!' cried Lucas. 'Look out, he's got a gun!'

Den stamped on the brakes and wrenched the steering wheel over to his left. At that moment a yellow spark flickered from the revolver and the windscreen of the Rolls disintegrated. Den struggled with the car as it slithered across the soft shoulder of the motorway and hit an RAC box. A second bullet thudded into the car, blowing away the side of Den Roberts' face. Then the Rover accelerated towards Birmingham.

'Are you all right?' whimpered Lucas. 'Den, are you all right? What's the matter with your –? Oh my God!'

Paul went down to breakfast feeling irritable. He had woken up with the knowledge that something was wrong, and it had taken him several seconds to remember what it was. Then it had dawned on him. As he dressed he peered casually out of the window, pretending not to expect the car to be parked in the mews. It wasn't.

Steve was already past the porridge and well into the bacon and eggs. Healthy breakfasts were her most serious character defect. She would follow with toast and marmalade. Paul tried not to notice. He went towards the door leading into the garage, but stopped himself. Instead he poured some black coffee.

'A bath and shave haven't done you much good,' said Steve.

'They wouldn't help to get the car back,' he said. 'The Rolls was stolen last night if you remember.'

'I know, I've been reading about it.' She tossed the newspaper across to him. 'You see, they've used that old photograph of you looking like a lean and glamorous bloodhound.'

Paul read the item: 'Mr Temple, usually so self-possessed, was highly irritable when our reporter spoke to him last night about the stolen car. "Don't ask me what happened", snapped Britain's number one Private Eye, "I haven't a clue." The police are treating this as a routine case . . .' He looked up at the spluttering sound coming from Steve.

'I never said that,' he complained. 'I never said a word about not having a –'

Kate Balfour bustled in from the tiny hall. 'Sorry to interrupt, Mr Temple, but Inspector Vosper is asking to see you.'

'Vosper?' he stared at the housekeeper in disbelief. 'But Charlie Vosper wouldn't be on a routine case of –' He stopped as she gestured that the inspector was standing behind her. 'Oh well, ask him to come in, will you, Kate?'

Vosper made his way directly to the coffee and sat at the table beside a spare cup. 'Good morning, Temple. That's very welcome, yes, I'll have white with three lumps, please. Good morning, Mrs Temple.' He was obviously pleased with himself. Either he had bad news for Paul or his retirement was due next week.

'So what news about my car?' asked Paul.

'Ah yes, your car. A sad business when you can't leave a Rolls Royce parked all evening in a London street, isn't it?' His grey eyes glittered maliciously. 'How many thousand pounds does a car like that cost? Or was that the one you were given as a bribe?'

'It was offered as an inducement for me to accept a case,' Paul agreed stiffly. 'But I paid the price for it when my wife

11

wouldn't let me return it. My wife enjoys sitting in the back making plans for new ways to furnish it.'

Vosper finished his coffee and then said casually, 'Well, we found it late last night, but it needs more than new furnishings. I'm afraid there was a very bad accident the other side of Newport Pagnell.'

'Tell me more,' Paul said with a glance at Steve.

'We found it in a ditch beside the M1. The car seems to have left the road, hit an RAC telephone box and then rolled down the bank. The radiator is damaged and the windscreen smashed.'

'Any trace of the driver?'

'I'm afraid so,' said Vosper. 'He was still at the wheel, with a bullet through his head. I forgot to mention the mess on the upholstery.'

Steve had risen to her feet. 'Oh, Paul!' She turned away and began pouring more coffee. 'So that's why you're here.'

'Who was the man?' Paul asked. 'Do you know him?'

'Yes, we know him. He was a small-time car thief called Den Roberts. There were fake number plates in the back of the car; I daresay he planned to change them over in Birmingham.'

'Was Roberts alone in the car?'

'He was alone when we found him.'

Paul thought for a moment. Roberts may have quarrelled with his accomplice, although it seemed unlikely that anybody would shoot the driver of the car he was travelling in. It was a problem.

'What's happened to my car now?' asked Paul.

'It's in the Pentagon Garage at Newport Pagnell. They'll telephone you when it's repaired.' Charlie Vosper raised himself ponderously from the chair, picked up his plain clothes trilby and announced with deliberation that it was all go, wasn't it? 'If there's nothing else, Temple. . .'

'I'll see you out.'

Paul took the inspector into the passage and closed the kitchen door. He glanced up the stairs behind him to the main part of the house, to make sure that Kate Balfour wasn't listening. 'Charlie,' said Paul, 'there's just one thing.'

'And what would that be?'

'This man Roberts. I wondered – could he have been mistaken for me?'

Vosper was surprised. 'Well, he wasn't much like you to look at, but it happened at night. Anybody overtaking the car might have been under the impression . . . I suppose it's possible. Do you think it was an attempt on your life, Temple?'

'No,' Paul said lightly, 'I haven't an enemy in the world. But let me know if there are more developments.'

He watched Inspector Vosper pad away down the cobbled mews and turn into Chester Square. Then Paul went back into the kitchen. He smiled reassuringly at Steve and began pouring more coffee.

'We'll have to book up for Geneva or the Highlands of Scotland this morning –'

'Darling, I suppose it didn't occur to Inspector Vosper that whoever shot the car thief might have been under the impression they were shooting you?'

'Good Lord, Steve, whatever put that idea into your head?'

'Don't tell me Britain's number one Private Eye didn't think of that one,' she said seriously. 'It was your car, in the dark, and the number plates hadn't been changed. Anyone following the car must have thought you were driving it.'

'You're being fanciful, darling. I expect you're worried about travelling by bus for the next week or so.' The telephone rang at that moment and Paul hoped it would be somebody to take Steve's mind off the subject.

13

'Mr Temple!' called Kate Balfour. 'It's Scott Reed for you!'

'I'll take it up in the workroom,' said Paul.

'Yes, it was a classic story of its kind – I sat up until three o'clock. Couldn't put it down. Absolutely riveting, although I still don't know who committed the murder. Was that intentional?

'But it will keep me solvent for another year,' Scott Reed concluded. 'Might even pay for this academic study of history and the myth of potency which I've just published.'

'What was that about?' Paul asked politely.

'I've no idea.'

Paul sat in the swivel chair at his desk and swung round with his feet in the air. Scott was a difficult man to keep to the point. And the idea of a scholarly work proving that politicians were national sex symbols seemed absurd.

'Before you ring off, Scott,' he interrupted, 'hang on, I want to ask you about Carl Milbourne. What made you think I'd want to get involved? Is there something mysterious about his death?'

'Good lord, no,' Scott said nervously. 'He was a friend of mine, that's all, and naturally when his wife told me she needed to talk to a skilled investigator –'

Paul laughed. 'I don't believe you, but it doesn't matter. Steve is dragging me off on holiday at the end of the week. You're a devious old devil. We'll see you when we come back.'

He replaced the receiver and swung his chair round to the desk as Kate Balfour tapped on the door. She showed in a dramatically attractive woman. Paul didn't need telling that this was the ex-actress widow of Carl Milbourne. She was dressed in mauve and she swept in with the distraught air that had thrilled gallery first-nighters in play after play during the post war years. She began pouring out her troubles as Paul was shaking her gloved hand.

'It's no use, Mr Temple,' she said tensely, sitting in the chair which Paul had indicated and peeling off the gloves, 'the more I think about it the more certain I am that the dead man we saw that morning was not my husband.'

Paul nodded sympathetically and asked why she hadn't said so at the time.

'I was upset. Confused.' A rapid glance at Paul and then she looked down again at the hands in her lap. 'I really didn't know what was happening.'

'But your brother was with you, Mrs Milbourne, and he also identified the body. Surely he wouldn't have –'

'Maurice was upset too,' she intruded. Her tone suddenly changed. 'You mean you've seen Maurice? You've been talking to him?'

'My wife and I had dinner out last night – at L'Hachoire Restaurant. Your brother was there, and he invited us into his office for a drink.'

'What did he say about me?' she asked suspiciously.

'He said that you were still very upset, Mrs Milbourne, and that you simply refuse to face up to your husband's death.' Paul sat on the sofa next to her. 'I didn't know your husband well, Mrs Milbourne. I only met him once, and that was several years ago. I don't believe he was married then.'

'We were married six years ago.'

'I remember him as a very charming man. I'm not surprised you find it difficult to imagine a world without him. You must feel very lonely now. I gather you don't have any children?'

Margaret Milbourne had acted in enough problem dramas to understand the significance of Paul's question. 'That's true. We both wanted children, but it wasn't to be.' She

15

sighed. 'Mr Temple, you might think this business has been too much for me and that I'm perhaps – a little unbalanced. But I assure you –'

'Don't worry about what I think, Mrs Milbourne. For the moment let's concentrate on the facts. What was your husband doing in Geneva?'

She was slightly pained by the efficient manner. 'Carl went on business, to see Julia Carrington.'

Paul knew the legend of Julia Carrington, the beautiful American actress who had retired after her tenth film and taken her dollars to Switzerland. Scandals still attached to her name as the dream factory hinted at indiscipline on the set and orgies between films.

'Carl had heard a rumour that she was writing her memoirs,' explained Margaret Milbourne. 'He was anxious to find out whether that was true.'

Yes, he would have been, Paul reflected. Julia Carrington's memoirs would be a scoop for any publisher. A success and sex story with famous names thrown in. Beautiful women, temperamental stars and bankers with several millions of dollars at stake. The only people who could be more interested in them than a publisher would be the famous names, the film company and the bankers.

'I didn't want him to go,' Margaret Milbourne was saying. 'I had a feeling, I don't know why. Julia Carrington doesn't bring other people luck. She has a doomed aura –'

'Mrs Milbourne, I don't doubt your sincerity. I don't doubt that you really believe that your husband is still alive. But feelings and aura and the word of a medium are not evidence.'

She smiled ironically. 'I have evidence.' She took a piece of paper from her handbag and passed it across to Paul. 'Is this evidence enough for you, Mr Temple?'

When she and her brother had returned from Switzerland after the accident Mrs Milbourne had found a parcel waiting at her home. It was addressed to Carl Milbourne from a shop in St Moritz. It contained the hat which Milbourne had been wearing when he left.

'Your husband's hat?' Paul repeated.

'Carl had a weakness for buying hats, he was constantly buying them. His dress sense was something I never quite adjusted to, even after six years of marriage. I knew at once what had happened. Carl had bought a new hat in St Moritz, and he had asked the shop to post his old one home.'

'But obviously,' Paul murmured, 'this must have happened before the accident.'

She raised an imperious hand. 'I'm coming to that, Mr Temple. You see, the hat was no use to me and I gave it away. I gave it to the gardener, as a matter of fact. And the day before yesterday he came to see me. He had found this piece of paper in the brim of the hat.'

Paul examined the paper. It was a note, dated January the sixth. 'Please don't worry,' it read. 'Have seen Randolph and everything will be all right. Will contact you later.' Paul looked enquiringly at Mrs Milbourne.

'January the sixth, Mr Temple, was two days after the accident.'

He nodded. 'Are you sure this is your husband's handwriting?'

'Positive.'

'So who do you suppose was killed by that car, Mrs Milbourne?'

'I haven't the remotest idea.'

Paul sighed. 'And I suppose you don't know anyone called Randolph. All we know is that whoever this note was addressed to it was never sent, otherwise it wouldn't have been in your husband's hat.'

'You're the private investigator, Mr Temple.'

Paul winced. She made him sound like a man in a raincoat spying on adulterers. One of these days, when he was grey and sporting a beard, he would call himself a criminologist. 'What did you want me to do, Mrs Milbourne?'

'I'd like you and Mrs Temple to come out with me to Switzerland.' She continued in a puzzled tone, 'I'd like to know what Carl was doing in St Moritz. He didn't tell me he was going there, and he hates winter sports.'

They were interrupted by the ringing of the telephone. 'Excuse me,' murmured Paul. He picked up the receiver.

'Is that Paul Temple?' asked the anxious voice. 'Darling, you won't remember me –'

'Dolly! Of course I remember you. How's the dancing now? Are you working again?' He shrugged apologetically at Mrs Milbourne. 'Oh dear, I'm sorry to hear that. Is there anything I can do?'

'I'd like to talk to you, Mr Temple, darling. It's terribly important.'

'Of course. Why don't you come round –?'

'No no,' the voice said anxiously, 'I'd sooner meet you somewhere else. In the open somewhere, the park or somewhere like that.'

'The Zoo?'

'That's a wonderful idea! Just the place! I'll be inside the main gate in about forty minutes. See you then, darling.'

Paul replaced the receiver and turned back to Mrs Milbourne. 'I'm sorry, an old friend of mine seems to be in trouble.'

'That's all right, Mr Temple,' she said. 'I rather think we've finished, haven't we? I'll arrange the flight –'

'There is one more thing. A personal question. Did you and your husband quarrel before he left for Geneva?'

She laughed dismissively. 'Actually, yes we did. I suppose Maurice told you?' She rose to her feet and began putting on her gloves. 'There was only one subject we ever quarrelled about, but unfortunately it happened to crop up just before he left. Carl was anxious to avoid paying death duties. He always took it for granted that he would go first, and . . .' Her voice quickened dramatically. 'He just would insist on talking about death. I hated the subject, simply hated it, Mr Temple. I used to tell him, "You're only forty-eight!" But he would insist on discussing it.'

'He talked about death and estate duties the night before he left for Geneva?' Paul asked thoughtfully.

'Yes, he did.'

Chapter Two

Paul Temple paid off his taxi outside the main entrance to the London Zoological Gardens. It was an exhilarating January morning with a low sun filtering through the clouds. Paul went in and bought a bag of peanuts for the monkeys; they deserved a treat in this temperature, although they looked perfectly cheerful.

The last time Paul had seen Dolly Brazier she had been in the dock for her part in a drugs scandal. He had known her for many years. She had played the part of a pop singer in a stage thriller he had written. The play had been a disaster, because the director had cut out most of the clues and all the explanations, but Dolly had remained his friend. A few years later when she was arrested Paul had persuaded Arnold Waldron to defend her, and Arnold had got her off with a twelve months' suspended sentence.

There was no sign of her yet, so Paul found a telephone kiosk and put through a call to the Pentagon Garage in Newport Pagnell. The drive across London with a talkative cockney taxi driver had convinced Paul that he needed the Rolls.

The news was unpromising. His car had been returned to the factory for a new radiator, a new windscreen and some panel beating. The cheerful indifference of the mechanic was tiresome, especially when he concluded that it would be about ten days before the work was completed. Paul hung up and went back to feed the monkeys.

'Hello, Paul! Here I am, darling!'

Dolly Brazier ran up through the west tunnel waving her handbag. She was a vivacious little red-head with a black maxi coat billowing to reveal the shapely legs of a chorus girl. She embraced him and left a smear of lipstick on his cheek.

'Nice to see you again,' said Paul. 'Although you don't look worried out of your mind to me.' She had that kind of face. 'Where are you working these days?'

'Oh, I've done all sorts of things since the summer season in Scarborough last year.' She laughed and took his arm. 'I even did secretarial work, until they discovered that I couldn't spell.'

'You haven't answered my question,' said Paul. 'Where are you working now?'

She tried to sound casual. 'I'm – you know, I'm a night club hostess. It's work, isn't it?'

'Where?'

'Oh, in Soho.' She took a peanut and threw it to a weary orang-utan. 'Shall we go across to the cafe by the penguin pool? I'm dying for a coffee.'

They walked across the gardens, past the screeching gibbons, the lions and the love-lorn panda, until they reached the refreshment stall. Paul bought two coffees and a packet of chocolate biscuits for Dolly.

'Now,' he said when they were sat down in full view of the penguins, 'you're working in a Soho club and you're in trouble. Tell me more.'

'Oh no, I didn't mean I was in trouble, darling. I'm worried about you. I mean, you've always been very kind to me, even though I was murdered in the first act of your play, and – well, you're in awful danger. Listen, Mr Temple, I wish you wouldn't get mixed up in this Swiss affair.'

'You mean Mrs Milbourne and –'

'I don't want to see anything happen to you, or that wife of yours. She was always terribly sweet and . . .' Her voice broke off incoherently.

'Do you know Mrs Milbourne, Dolly?'

'No,' she said. 'But I've heard of her, in a roundabout way. She's been talking to you, claiming that her husband isn't dead.' She put her hand on Paul's. 'Are you going to help her?'

Paul shrugged. 'She only spoke to me this morning.'

'Well, don't help her, Mr Temple. Don't get involved, darling, it isn't worth it'

'I'm grateful to you for being so concerned,' Paul said, slightly amused, 'but you know, Steve and I have come up against a few ruthless people in our time. We're still alive to tell the tale.'

Dolly cast a nervous glance over her shoulder. 'Well, you can't say I didn't warn you. I'd never have forgiven myself if I hadn't passed the word. But I must get back. If I'm seen with you –'

'But you haven't passed any word, Dolly! You haven't told me a damn thing.' As he walked beside her towards the south gate he asked, 'Is Carl Milbourne dead? Was he really killed in that accident?'

'I don't know,' she said. 'I don't know anything about Carl Milbourne. All I know is that – that a certain person doesn't want you to help Mrs Milbourne.'

'Who, Dolly?' He took her by the shoulders and made her look at him. 'Why won't you tell me all you know?'

'Because I'm scared.' She smiled helplessly. 'You see, darling, I'm too young to die. I'm sorry.' She broke away from him and ran out of the gate.

Paul wandered down past the wolves, deep in thought. There were too many things he needed to know, such as whether the man killed in the car had been alone and whether there were witnesses to the accident. Paul liked the wolves, they were elegant and wild, and they didn't smell so strongly in winter. He admired the one standing guard on the top of the air raid shelter. Supposing the dead man were not Carl Milbourne, Paul reflected. Did that mean Milbourne had arranged an accident so that he could disappear? In which case, as somebody's body had definitely been dead, was Milbourne involved in murder?

Paul glanced at his watch. Nearly twelve o'clock. He decided to telephone Steve and ask her to meet him for an early lunch.

Kate Balfour watched from the kitchen window as a black Wolseley drew up in the mews. She heard Steve come down the stairs and answer the door herself.

'Mrs Temple? My name's Stone, of the Pentagon Garage.'

'Oh yes,' she heard Steve say, 'you have my husband's car.'

'That's right, Mrs Temple. But it will take a couple of weeks to put right, so your husband has hired this for the meantime.'

Kate was an ex-policewoman and it pleased her to see that Paul would be driving something more appropriate than the Rolls. In her day all black Wolseleys were police cars and she knew their performance. Not that Mr Stone looked like a policeman. He was standing by the car with Steve, handing over the keys and pointing out the logbook.

'Kate,' said Steve excitingly. 'I'm just off to meet Paul for lunch. I'm mobile again.'

'Yes, Mrs Temple.'

As Kate watched Stone walk off towards Chester Square the Wolseley shuddered and then purred gently away.

Beautiful cars, she thought, what a shame the police are driving about in any old vehicle these days; all those blue flashing lights and vulgar klaxons. Her reverie was interrupted by the telephone ringing.

'Hello, Kate. Is my wife there?'

'No, Mr Temple, she's just left in the new car to meet you for lunch.'

'Oh good, she must be psychic.' There was a pause at the other end of the line. 'What did you say about a new car?'

'From the Pentagon Garage, the one you hired. It was delivered a few minutes ago and Mrs Temple went straight off-'

'The Pentagon Garage is in Newport Pagnell, Kate. I didn't hire a car from them or anybody else!'

Kate Balfour slammed down the telephone and ran from the house. She had her mini in the mews and she set off in pursuit as if she had klaxons blaring and blue lights flashing. She nipped round Chester Square and through the streets of Chelsea with angry motorists aghast and hooting in her wake. Which way Steve had gone was sheer guesswork, but Kate assumed she would have gone up Kensington Church Street, through Sussex Gardens and along Marylebone Road. There was only one recent change in the traffic system, but Kate found herself doing forty miles an hour in the wrong direction along the new one-way street towards a bus. She gritted her teeth and decided to let the bus driver have a heart attack. Kate was in too much of a hurry to lose a game of chicken.

The bus veered into a garage entrance and frightened a postman. Kate sped on, jumping traffic lights where necessary and waving the occasional V-sign at self-important taxi drivers. She had reached Baker Street and was beginning to think she had come the wrong way when she saw the black Wolseley at the lights ahead.

Kate went round an island into the wrong side of the road and drove on. With a hand pressed firmly on the hooter she kept going until a bus came nose to nose with her, then she jumped out and ran the twenty yards more to the black Wolseley.

'Hey, missis, that's no place to park while you do your shopping,' bawled the bus driver. Four taxi drivers joined in the chorus.

Kate pulled open the Wolseley door as Steve was about to drive off. 'Come out of that car, Steve,' she said urgently. 'There may be a bomb –'

Steve nipped out quickly, without any flustered argument. That was what Kate admired about her, she was both attractive *and* sensible. She argued afterwards. 'Car hire firms wouldn't be so careless,' she began.

'Mr Temple telephoned soon after you left and said he hadn't ordered a car!'

There were two commotions now: one doing nicely in front of the abandoned mini and another starting up behind the Wolseley. A policeman was padding purposefully towards them. 'What's going on?' he was demanding. 'You can't leave a car in the middle of the road like this!' The crowds on the pavement were stopping to watch the fun and a traffic warden was threading her menacing way through the jam.

'Wait in the mini, dear,' said Kate. 'I'll dump the Wolseley round the corner.'

'Madam, you're obstructing the traffic,' the policeman insisted. 'You'll have to move that car immediately.'

'I'd like to examine it first,' said Kate. 'I have reason to believe –' The bonnet of the car lifted suddenly, there was a

26

crash of tearing metal and the front of the Wolseley exploded. Steve ducked instinctively. There were pieces of steel scattering in every direction, smashing windows and cutting into other cars. A taxi driver fell to the ground beside his cab. It seemed nearly half a minute between the hideous bang and the eventual silence which followed. Then somebody screamed, the taxi driver began to curse to himself, and the people on the pavements moved forward among the metal and broken glass.

Steve looked appealingly comic sitting up in bed with a piratical bandage across her forehead. The urchin grin she gave as Paul burst into the bedroom was apologetic. But Paul was too shocked to be amused. He sat on the bed tight lipped and anxious.

'How are you now, Steve?'

'Darling, I'm perfectly all right. I've a slight headache which would disappear if you'd let me get up and make a pot of tea.'

'Kate is already making tea.'

Steve looked slightly bashful. 'Is Kate all right?'

'Of course she's all right, she's an ex-policewoman. A little shaken up to begin with, but I increased her salary and she brightened up at once. The only other casualty was a taxi driver, and he was discharged from hospital as soon as they'd stuck some elastoplasts on his knee. So relax, stay in bed and be pampered.'

Kate came bustling in with tea and biscuits. The whiff of crime was obviously in her nostrils – the tea was not of her usual standard and while it had been standing she had telephoned the Pentagon Garage to establish that they didn't know a Mr Stone.

'Well, we had to check,' said Paul. 'Perhaps you'd have another go at contacting Mrs Milbourne?'

'Yes, Mr Temple,' and she bustled out.

'Paul, what happened this morning?'

He poured the tea and passed her a cup. 'This morning?' he repeated innocently.

'With Dolly Brazier.'

'Oh, she tried to borrow some money from me. Poor Dolly, she's always in some kind of trouble.'

'Did you lend it to her?'

'Of course not. She wanted a hundred pounds, and you know how these things develop. Once you start lending people money –'

'I don't believe a word of it,' Steve interrupted. 'If Dolly had needed money you'd have lent it to her. I know you, Paul. What did she really want?'

Paul rearranged the flowers he had brought for her. They were gladioli and he wondered absently where flowers came from at this time of year. 'She told me to take care,' he said quietly. 'Not to become involved.' Perhaps they were imported from the Bahamas. If they have gladioli in the Bahamas.

'Involved in what?' Steve asked. 'In the Milbourne affair?'

'I didn't intend to tell you about this, Steve,' he said. 'Not today. You need to rest –'

'I'll rest when I know what's going on. I have to be kept in the picture, and you just remember that, Temple!'

Paul laughed and said, 'Of course I will, darling.' He kissed her and ruffled her hair so that it partially covered the bandage. 'I'll rest better myself when I know what's going on.' He went to the door and blew her a kiss. 'Sleep well, darling.'

He found Kate in his workroom, sitting at his desk and talking briskly on the telephone. Daunting, Paul thought to himself, she must have routed crime like a battleship in her day. He had a brief mental picture of her tossing gangsters across the police station, reducing full grown bruisers to tears.

'No lead there, Mr Temple,' she said as she hung up. 'Mrs Milbourne didn't tell anyone about her visit, except her brother. She hasn't seen many people socially since her husband –'

'I'm not surprised. Kate, will you stay and keep an eye on my wife for a couple of hours? I think I'd better visit Mrs Milbourne's brother. And after that I might find out a little more about Dolly Brazier's current job.'

Maurice Lonsdale greeted him like an old friend and insisted that they should dine together. 'So much more civilised than talking in the office,' he said. 'I'm told the trout is superb this week.'

Paul agreed to sample the trout.

'I'm glad you saw my sister, Temple.' He had a good memory and ordered the dry sherry Paul had had the last time. 'But I hope you didn't take her story too seriously. You see, Margaret has always been highly strung, even when she was in the theatre.'

'Apart from being highly strung,' said Paul, 'she's also highly intelligent. I don't think we can completely dismiss everything she says.'

'Good gracious me, of course not,' he said quickly. 'I'm not suggesting we should, Temple. Not for one minute. But I did go out to Switzerland with her. I saw Carl after the accident and I identified him.' He paused while the waiter placed the soup before them. 'However, you're a busy man. I'm sure you had a particular reason for coming to see me this evening.'

Paul nodded. 'I want to know who else you've discussed this business with. Who, apart from your sister, knows that I've been consulted?'

'A curious question,' he murmured thoughtfully.

'An important one.'

Lonsdale thought for a moment. 'I may have mentioned you casually to some friends or acquaintances when we were talking about my sister. I would have seen no reason for not doing so.' He tipped the bowl in the wrong direction to reach the last spoonful of soup. 'Why is it so important?'

'Because,' Paul said grimly, 'while my wife and I were talking to you last night my car was stolen. The man who stole it was shot – in mistake for me. And at lunchtime today there was a deliberate attempt to kill my wife.'

Lonsdale stared in amazement. As he blinked it looked as if he were lowering shutters over the cold grey eyes to keep out the truth. 'And you think that both these –'

'I think that someone is deliberately trying to stop me taking an interest in the Milbourne case.'

Lonsdale shook his head and muttered, 'No, it's not possible. No, never.' He pushed the empty plate aside and looked again at Paul. 'There's only one person, but she's the soul of discretion. I discussed my sister and the car accident at length with a very good friend of mine, and I remember I did mention you. She had read several of your books –'

'Could you tell me her name?'

'Freda Sands.'

Paul had heard of Freda Sands. She ran a secretarial bureau in Baker Street, and whenever highly successful business-women were needed by television or press interviewers they contrived to interview her. She was dynamic, attractive, and she didn't believe in the equality of the sexes because she knew she was superior to any man. She made good copy and she photographed well. Paul wondered where she found the time to read his books.

'You must meet her,' said Lonsdale, 'I'm sure both you and Mrs Temple would enjoy her company. I'll arrange a little dinner party one evening.'

'That would be pleasant,' Paul murmured.

He was wondering whether this was the flaw in Lonsdale's character – the social ambitions of a millionaire to know and be seen with the fashionable people of the moment. As Paul was thinking this through the waiter approached the table with a message.

'Excuse me, Mr Lonsdale,' he said, 'but I have a message for Mr Temple. An Inspector Vosper telephoned. He wants to see you immediately, sir, at the Middlesex Hospital.'

'Did he say why?' asked Paul, rising in alarm.

'No, sir. But it sounded urgent.'

Lonsdale rose to his feet as well. 'Gaston, send my chauffeur round to the entrance. I'm sorry, Temple, I hope it's nothing to do with your wife's accident. My chauffeur will run you to the hospital in ten minutes.'

'That's very kind of you.'

Charlie Vosper was sitting in the corridor of the casualty wing, smoking an impatient cigarette under a No Smoking notice when Paul arrived. He stubbed out the cigarette on the gleaming floor. 'So you got my message,' he said. 'I telephoned your home and Detective Sergeant Balfour –'

'You mean Kate,' he interrupted. 'What's happened? Who has been hurt?'

'About an hour ago one of our people found a woman called Dolly Brazier in a cul-de-sac off the Kilburn High Road. She'd been very severely done over, I'm afraid.'

'How severely?' Paul snapped.

'Very,' he sighed. 'I don't suppose she's going to die, but

31

that isn't everything, is it? She was obviously an attractive girl before –' He smiled sadly. 'The poor kid's only spoken twice, and on both occasions she asked for you.'

Paul went into the tiny ward. He scarcely heard the doctor say something about having given her an injection. He moved the screen aside and sat by the bed. The brutality of her attackers made him feel sick.

'Can you hear me, Dolly?' he asked softly. 'It's Paul.'

Her hand moved slightly and Paul took it in his. A plastic bag was connected to her arm transfusing blood, and her face was swathed in white dressings. The room was silent except for Dolly's laboured breathing beneath the broken ribs.

'Who was it?' he asked. 'Who did this to you, Dolly?'

'I don't know,' she whispered.

'You must tell me,' Paul said firmly. 'I'll make sure nothing else happens to you –'

But she wasn't listening. 'I'm going to get better, aren't I, Paul? I'm too young to die –'

'Don't be silly, of course you're going to get better.' He squeezed her hand and waited for her to recover herself. She seemed to have that phrase, 'too young to die', firmly lodged in her mind. It was the second time she had used it.

'I asked the doctor about my face,' she said, speaking with difficulty. 'About the stitches. But he wouldn't tell me anything. Is it a mess, Paul?'

'You'll soon be beautiful again,' he said with false cheerfulness. 'It's a bit of a mess now, but you're in good hands. Just be a good girl and tell me why you were attacked.'

Eventually she whispered, 'I told you, keep out of this affair. You mustn't. . .'

The nurse tapped Paul on the shoulder and indicated that his time was up. Dolly had fallen asleep and the drug would keep her that way for several hours. There was no sense, he thought, in such savagery, no necessity at all.

'She'll be all right, Mr Temple,' said the house doctor as they left the ward. 'But her head wounds are rather delicate so we have to take care.'

'Of course,' said Paul. 'Do everything you can for her, please. I'll pay whatever is necessary, and if it's a question of plastic surgery phone Sir Thomas Staines, he's a friend of mine.'

'Don't worry, Mr Temple.'

Don't worry. Paul went off down the corridor. His footsteps echoed and in the distance trolleys and pans made noises that reverberated through the tiled passages. Hospitals were full of impersonal sounds at night. No, he wouldn't worry. The lift gates clattered and he left Dolly Brazier five floors behind. It read 'Theatre' on the signboard for Dolly's floor.

She had told Paul not to worry, throughout rehearsals and even after the appalling reviews. Don't worry, darling, it's your first play, you can always write another one. She had been a resilient, happy kid. Loyal and affectionate. She didn't deserve to end up in a heap behind the Kilburn High Road.

Paul stepped into the road and waved down a taxi.

Chapter Three

Margaret Milbourne said good evening to the commissionaire as he held open the door. It was ten past six, an appropriate ten minutes late. She didn't approve of punctuality, it cheapened one so, however anxious she was to meet this mysterious Danny what's-his-name. As she walked through the foyer she glanced at the wall mirror and lifted her head a shade higher. It was important to look serene in the midst of tragedy.

Danny Clayton, that was his name. He had sounded young and American on the telephone, and he had some information about her husband. She pushed through the swing doors to the cocktail bar. A smattering of customers, a desultory air of opulence, and a forlorn man playing muzack at the piano. She thought it should be possible to recognise Danny Clayton by instinct – he would be the slim, hawk nosed youth who was watching the other customers with something like amused contempt.

'Can I get you anything?' asked the barman.

'Not for the moment, thank you,' she said. 'I'm meeting a Mr Clayton. I believe he's staying here.'

He was the slim, hawk nosed youth. He ordered drinks and guided Margaret across to a corner seat. His absentminded good manners unnerved her slightly. He said it was good of her to spare the time, but he spoke with such casual insincerity that she couldn't think how to reply.

'Who are you exactly?' she asked. 'What do you want?'

'I'm Danny Clayton, I'm thirty years old, I was born in New York, I work for Julia Carrington, and I wanted to see you about your husband.'

Was that supposed to be funny or downright rude? 'Julia Carrington?' she repeated, clutching at the familiar name and hoping to slow him down.

'I'm Julia's confidential secretary,' he said with a laugh, 'among other things. I'm also her business adviser, whipping boy and general yes-man. Julia has given me the sack five times and I've walked out on her more often than I care to remember. She's a bitch, Mrs Milbourne, but luckily for me a very generous bitch.'

His dress was very English, modern English, thought Margaret, but young people's styles were so confusing these days. She looked at his long hair (she would have called it a page boy cut) and his shirt with matching tie. 'What has all this to do with my husband, Mr Clayton?'

'He came to see Julia just before the accident.'

'I know. That's why he went to Switzerland in the first place, to see your Miss Carrington.'

'Right, only he didn't see her.' Danny Clayton laughed apologetically. 'He saw me instead.'

'I wish you'd get to the point,' she said distractedly. Her serenity was slipping away and she could do nothing about it. 'What did you want to tell me about my husband?'

'Mrs Milbourne, I have one or two photographs in my wallet.' He produced his wallet and drew out the photographs like a conjuror. 'I'd like you to take a look at these.'

The photographs were of her husband, wearing a strange new hat in St Moritz. The photographer's name and date stamp were on the back – they were taken on January the sixth.

'Can I have another martini?' she asked.

Clayton crooked his finger at a passing waiter.

'What was Carl doing in St Moritz? And if he wasn't killed in that car accident why did he let me think that he had been?' She was almost in tears. But Clayton's reply brought her back to crude reality.

'I can answer those questions, Mrs Milbourne. I can answer any questions you care to ask me about your husband, but I'm afraid this is going to cost you a lot of money.'

She felt as if he had kicked her in the stomach. 'You mean this is blackmail?'

Paul Temple was on the telephone when Mrs Milbourne was shown into the workroom. It was nine o'clock and he had been listening patiently to Scott Reed for half an hour. 'Yes, Scott, I always talk to journalists about avenging angels coming in to restore normality. That's right, a sudden melo-dramatic action disrupts the community, but it can be put right by logical thinking and an eye for the shady butler.' Scott had remembered the highbrow interview and he didn't want Paul to be too casually modest.

'Don't forget to mention your theories on the identity of Jack the Ripper,' said Scott. 'She'll have heard of Jack the Ripper.'

'I forget what my last theory was.'

He let Scott prattle on while Steve was looking after Mrs Milbourne. They seemed to be discussing Steve's afternoon at Scotland Yard looking through the 'mug book' to identify Mr Pentagon Garage. Mrs Milbourne appeared none too reassured to hear of the exploding car and the fate of Dolly Brazier.

'Have you ever heard of Dolly Brazier?' Paul asked when eventually he had disposed of his publisher.

'No, but of course it's a scandal when a young girl can't –'

'Quite. Does the name Freda Sands mean anything to you?'

Mrs Milbourne looked startled. 'Yes, of course. She's a great friend of my brother's.'

'Did your husband know her?'

'Yes, quite well,' she said distractedly. 'Miss Sands often supplied him with typists and office staff.'

Steve had noticed the edge to Margaret's voice. 'Is she a friend of yours, Mrs Milbourne?'

'No. I should imagine that most of Freda's friends are men, preferably men who can put business her way. That's how she's done so well, of course.'

There was a pause. Paul wondered why Mrs Milbourne had come to see him. She didn't seem anxious to come to the point.

'I always had the impression she had her eye on Carl,' she was saying. 'Carl used to laugh at me for suggesting such a thing, but you know how it is, Mrs Temple. A woman can have an intuition about these things.'

'I know what you mean,' Steve said with a laugh.

How would she know anything of the kind, Paul wondered. 'Brandy?' he asked. 'Then you can tell me why you've arrived with such an appearance of urgency. Has something happened?'

Margaret Milbourne hesitated, glanced at herself in the mirror as if she were making an entrance, then launched into an account of her meeting with Danny Clayton. 'I felt as if he'd kicked me in the stomach,' she said indignantly.

An inelegant phrase, but Paul listened with fascination. This was a development he would not have expected. Even allowing for the dramatic embellishments which an actress would hardly resist (making Clayton speak and look like a B picture heavy) it seemed as if a serious attempt had been made at blackmail.

'He demanded five thousand pounds,' she said.

'But what exactly for?' Paul asked.

'I'm not sure. I suppose he'll tell me tomorrow. I'm supposed to visit him at eleven o'clock with five thousand pounds in used notes.'

'At the New Wilton Hotel?'

'No no, somewhere out in Berkshire.' She rummaged in her handbag until she found a used envelope with the address scribbled on the back. 'The Three Star Hotel, Bray-on-Thames.' She shrugged helplessly. 'It's near Maidenhead.'

Paul knew one man in London who had worked in Hollywood. When Mrs Milbourne had left he telephoned Vince Langham.

Actually Vince was the most important film director he knew. The film he had made of a Paul Temple novel many years ago was his least claim to fame, if only because he had just arrived in England in flight from McCarthy and had directed it under another name. But the film had been staggering, pulling Paul's story apart and turning it into a statement about man's barbarity to man. There had been a lot of symbolism, youths on motorbikes in an English village, phallic church spires and bells ringing ecstatically as the heroine was ravaged on Hallow'en. It had been the beginning of a new career for Vince, and the start of highbrow attention for Paul.

'He's directing a musical,' said Vince's wife. 'You'll find him at Victoria coach station.'

An army of film extras was piling into coaches – cut – piling out again, piling in, while cameramen and technicians and all those people with no ostensible job to do milled about among the confusion. Perched high above the scene with a megaphone was Vince Langham, the director. He required seven takes of the extras piling into the coach, and then the arc lamps and the cameras had to be moved to another part of the action. Vince Langham's perch was lowered to the ground.

'Twenty minutes,' bellowed Langham's assistant through a megaphone, 'everybody back in twenty minutes!'

Vince was a rugged man in his mid-fifties with unkempt hair straggling over the collar of his overcoat. Before he had become a director he had acted in several cowboy films and he still looked uncomfortable in modern dress.

'Good lord, Paul Temple,' he called as he jumped to the floor. 'Come and have coffee with me.' He led Paul to a mobile dressing room which he was using beneath the departures board. 'We've been four months on this epic and we're off the floor tonight, spot on schedule. Just re-shooting some of the crowd scenes.'

He talked for a while about the film, made the routine complaints about his bitch of a leading lady, and then asked what Paul was doing out at this time of night.

'I came here to ask about Julia Carrington,' said Paul. 'Last time I saw you I remember you were going to Switzerland to see her.'

'That's right. I had a wonderful vehicle for Julia, and I hoped I could lure her out of retirement.' He laughed. 'But I came up against some secretary of hers, and the little bastard advised her against playing the part.'

'Not a certain Mr Clayton, by any chance?' murmured Paul.

He looked surprised. 'That's right, Danny Clayton. Do you know him?'

'No,' said Paul, 'but I've heard a few things.'

Vince Langham needed no prompting to talk about Danny Clayton. 'A real young man on the make, all nerve and no talent,' was his opinion. 'But he seems to have sold his act to poor Julia. She thinks he's the original boy wonder.'

'Is he simply her secretary –?'

'He's every damn thing in her life. Even does her thinking for her.' Langham added brandy to his coffee and offered the flask to Paul. 'Do you know, this was a wonderful vehicle for Julia, absolutely made for her. I'd found this novel called *Too Young to Die* and it had everything. The very first scene –'

'I don't think I've read it,' Paul said thoughtfully, 'although it sounds familiar. Who wrote it?'

Vince hesitated. 'A guy called Randolph. Richard Randolph. I've never met him, but I expect he'll be on all the television chat shows next month when it's published.'

'Who,' Paul asked thoughtfully, 'is the publisher?'

'God knows, I can never remember names.' Vince waved aside the irrelevance. 'I obtained a copy from a friend of mine who saw it in typescript. She recognised it as a vehicle for Julia Carrington.' He sighed. 'And she was right, by God.'

'Who was this friend of yours?'

'A woman called Freda Sands. Her agency typed the novel, that was how she came to read it. She's a very remarkable woman –'

'So I've been hearing.'

'You seem to have been hearing a lot. What's happening, Temple? I know it's a bit unethical to get hold of a typescript before the publisher, but it goes on all the time. No need for an investigation. Some of the biggest film deals in movie history have been fixed that way.'

41

Somebody banged on the dressing room door. 'Everyone back in their place,' the assistant was shouting. 'Everyone on set!'

Vince grinned. 'I seem to be needed. Are you going to stay and watch, Paul?'

'No, I have to be up early in the morning. If you'd had a full orchestra out there in the coach bays it might have been different,' he said with a laugh. 'Your wife said this was a musical. But I'm going out to Bray-on-Thames first thing to see a man called Danny Clayton.'

'If you catch him with his back turned,' Vince said wryly, 'give him a kick in the pants from me.'

Chapter Four

The Three Star Hotel at Bray was on a bend in the river. Paul Temple stood watching the swans drift upstream; they bobbed gracefully as a motor launch swept past and caught them in its wash. It was a tranquil, cold morning and the sounds of traffic seemed very remote. Paul watched a fisherman along the bank wind in a roach that must have weighed at least seven pounds, then he turned and went through the glass doors into the bar.

'I'm meeting a Mr Danny Clayton,' he said to the landlord. 'He was going to be here at eleven o'clock.'

The American gentleman?' he said abruptly. 'He's left.'

The landlord was a veteran of the Battle of Britain. He stared at Paul. 'You're not Mr Temple?'

'Yes,' said Paul, 'my name's Temple.'

'Mr Clayton said you'd be calling. He left a note for you.' The landlord retrieved a note from beside the till. 'Mr Clayton had a reservation here, but he called in this morning and cancelled it. Probably found out that we don't sell Coca-Cola.'

Paul unfolded the message feeling that somebody had outsmarted him. He was being manipulated. Nobody except Margaret Milbourne had known he would be coming. . .

Dear Mr Temple, the message read, *If you are interested in what happened to Carl Milbourne I suggest that you meet me at Peter's Folly, which is a houseboat near Salter's End. I shall refuse to see you if you are accompanied by anyone. Danny Clayton.*

The landlord was peering over his shoulder. 'Salter's End is about half a mile down stream, Mr Temple. Can't miss it. Dozens of houseboats.'

'Who lives on Peter's Folly?'

'Chap called Peter, Peter Fletcher. He's an artist, so I suppose he can afford a few follies.' The landlord made it clear that Fletcher was a charlatan. 'Not that he'll be on the houseboat this morning. He has a flat in London.'

'You've been very helpful.' Paul smiled and tried to sound casual. 'I wonder whether you'd do me a favour? If I'm not back here in one hour could you telephone Inspector Jenkins of Bray CID?'

The landlord nodded. 'I wondered whether you were *the* Paul Temple. Well, you can rely on me, sir.'

Paul set off along the tow-path with only the lapping of the water and occasional fields of cows as company. A harsh breeze was cutting across the flat Berkshire countryside. He shivered, increased his pace, and tried to pretend that this would purge those centrally-heated weeks in London.

Yet he wondered what he was doing out here. Pursuing a blackmailer, perhaps, or trying to find a neurotic woman's husband. But the only way to find Carl Milbourne was to go to Switzerland and look into the accident, or try to discover who would benefit from his supposed death. Chasing after Danny Clayton wasn't the most direct lead in that direction. Although staying in England did make some sense: somebody had been playing games in England:

shooting up the Rolls, trying to blow up Steve, beating up Dolly Brazier. I'm here, Paul thought to himself, because I'm angry about those games.

He followed the bend of the river and came to the small inlet called Bidford Creek which was crowded with houseboats. They looked drab and deserted at this time of year. The only sign of life was at the far end where three police cars stood by the dirt path and blue uniforms were hurrying down to Peter's Folly.

'Sorry to stop you, sir,' said a constable as Paul hurried round the inlet. 'Would you mind telling me where you're going?'

'What's happened?' Paul demanded.

The constable blocked the tow-path. 'I'd be glad if you'd answer my question, sir.'

'I was looking for a houseboat called Peter's Folly, but it looks as though your people have found it first.'

The dapper figure of Inspector Jenkins came towards them. 'Hello, Temple,' he called officiously. 'I hope you're going to turn round and go straight back in the direction you came from? I couldn't bear another case in which my men do all the work while you prowl about behind my back being brilliant. Why not pop across the county border into Buckinghamshire?'

Paul chuckled as if the inspector were joking. 'That was five years ago, Emlyn. It's time you had another success in your career.'

'Another success? What do you want me to do, find your stolen car?' The quip kept him amused while they watched the ambulance bump noisily along the dirt path and stop by the houseboat. 'I cut out the press report on your car. It's pinned on the notice board in my office and whenever I'm feeling depressed I go and read it.'

The two old friends wandered across to the ambulance while Paul explained his reason for being there. They watched a stretcher swathed in blankets carried ashore.

'What's happened, Emlyn? Has there been an accident?'

'Not an accident,' said the inspector. 'Murder.'

'I've been having one of those weeks,' murmured Paul. 'Do you know the name of the victim?'

'Peter Fletcher, of course. It's his bloody houseboat, isn't it?'

'Yes,' Paul agreed, 'it's his houseboat. But I didn't necessarily expect it to be his body. The murderer is very wasteful.'

The inspector climbed into the ambulance and leaned over the stretcher. 'It's Peter Fletcher all right,' he said bitterly. 'We know him in these parts.' He flipped back the blanket and looked at the face. Somebody had closed the dead man's eyes, but the expression of pain and surprise remained fixed.

'What does the murderer waste?' asked Jenkins as he led the way up the gangplank and on to the boat. 'You said he was wasteful.'

'He wastes human life,' Paul said thoughtfully. 'And motor cars. He seems to be flailing about like a destructive child, without a sufficient motive. I call that wasteful.'

Jenkins grunted to himself. 'You can explain yourself later, when there's more time for philosophical discussion.' He lowered himself through the hatch into the living quarters of the boat.

There was a bunk right up forrard, and the galley was aft; the rest was all studio. The landlord of the Three Star Hotel had been correct – Peter Fletcher was a charlatan. All his paintings, and there were stacks of them against the bulwarks, were pretty landscapes of Thames scenes. They were rich in colour and slick in execution, autumnal and insensitive. He had clearly sold them by the yard to furniture shops.

'You see,' said Inspector Jenkins, 'he was an artist.'

'I should think he also worked in advertising.' On the drawing board was a sketch of a snow-capped hill with the text beside it – the cool crisp flavour of the English country-side in a menthol cigarette. 'He would normally have done this sort of thing in his office. Poor old Fletcher. What a shame he decided to do this sketch on location.'

'What makes you say that?'

'It cost him his life. Normally he painted here at weekends, but obviously he arrived this morning to do his cigarette sketch and gave someone a surprise.'

Jenkins stared blankly at the cool crisp flavour of the English countryside, then while he considered Paul's theory he lit a cigarette. 'You may be right,' he said eventually.

'Of course I'm right. How was Fletcher killed?'

'He was stabbed.' Jenkins sat on a bunk and rubbed his cold hands together before a paraffin stove. 'Someone apparently crept up behind him while he was . . .' His voice tailed off as professional suspicion took over. 'Now listen, Temple, you haven't told me why you were visiting Fletcher. Why did you have an appointment with him?'

Paul raised an admonishing finger. 'I didn't say my appointment was with Fletcher.'

'What I like about you, Temple, is that you never stoop to the obvious explanation. You never try to over-simplify, do you?'

'No.' Paul had been looking at the chalk-marked outline in the middle of the floor. It presumably showed where Fletcher's body had been found. There was still a pool of blood just outside the line. Fletcher had been face downwards and the wound in his back had bled profusely, down to his hips and then sideways on to the floor. 'Did you find the weapon?' Paul asked.

'No. I expect it's at the bottom of the river by now.'

Paul stood where Fletcher might have been standing when he died. Behind him was the door swinging open into the sleeping quarters. 'Who discovered the body?' he asked.

'A woman in the next houseboat. Name of Harrison. She thought she heard someone leaving the boat in a hurry so she looked out and saw the canopy flapping. Typical nosey woman, she didn't try to see who was leaving the boat, she just investigated the canopy and found the corpse. And don't ask me the next question. You want to know when this was.' Inspector Jenkins glanced at his self winding automatic watch with daily calendar and jewelled action. 'He seems to have died at about ten forty-five.'

A book on the serving hatch caught Paul's eye, firstly because it was the only book in the houseboat, and secondly because it was called *Too Young to Die*, by someone called Richard Randolph.

'What's this book doing here?' Paul demanded.

'I don't know,' said the inspector. 'The strangest people seem to read themselves to sleep. It isn't important –'

'Where did you find it?'

Jenkins struggled with his honour and then admitted, 'Now you mention it, I believe it was on the floor by the body when we arrived. Why? Does it matter?'

'Yes, this is a rather special book. For one thing it hasn't yet been published. It's an advance copy which they only send out to reviewers and people with a special interest in the subject. Whereabouts by the body did you find it?'

Inspector Jenkins pointed to the centre of the cabin, by the chalk mark which indicated the dead man's right hand.

'I thought as much,' said Paul. 'You know what happened here this morning, don't you?'

The inspector blinked, stubbed out his cigarette, and breathed deeply. 'No. Tell me what happened.'

'Fletcher came home unexpectedly this morning. He saw that book lying on the table and wondered where the devil it had come from.'

'You mean the book didn't belong to him?' Jenkins scratched the thin stubble of his moustache. 'That the book was planted?'

'That's right. Fletcher saw the book, was immediately curious, and did precisely what the murderer expected he would do. He turned his back on the partition and stooped down to pick up the book from the table. In my opinion the book was in his hands when he died.'

'Yes, that's very possible.' Jenkins grinned. 'You're probably right. Now all we have to do is find the murderer and we'll know it all, won't we?'

Paul knew enough already to realise that the book had been planted there to attract his own attention. *Too Young to Die* had been mentioned in some strange circumstances, and the killer hidden in the houseboat had known Paul would pick it up. He hadn't known that Fletcher would come in first.

'Don't touch it,' Jenkins snapped as Paul reached out for the book. 'We'll have to check that for fingerprints.'

'As long as you don't start arresting your own men, Emlyn. They've probably all thumbed through it since the first idiot moved it'

Heavy footsteps were coming up the gangplank. While Inspector Jenkins went to the hatch Paul used his handkerchief to flick open the tide page of the book. Yes, it was all fitting neatly together. *Too Young to Die* by Richard Randolph was published in London by Milbourne & Co. It was all very neat indeed.

'Excuse me, inspector,' the newcomer called down to them. 'We've had a message over the radio for you. The landlord of the Three Star Hotel in Bray has telephoned to say that Paul Temple is missing and probably in danger.'

Jenkins growled to himself that he had no such luck.

The fisherman was still sitting downstream from the hotel. Paul said, 'Good afternoon,' and woke him out of his trance. A lone swan was watching the catch of tantalising fish wriggling in the net. Paul went into the hotel to reassure the landlord of his survival.

'I hear there was trouble at the houseboat,' said the man. 'Somebody killed.'

'Fletcher,' said Paul.

'Oh.' The landlord looked thoughtful as he poured Paul a whisky. 'What happened to Mr Clayton?'

'You might well ask. There was no sign of him at Peter's Folly.' Paul helped himself to a turkey sandwich. 'What did Clayton look like?'

'You haven't met him?' the landlord asked in surprise. 'Well, he was a man of about forty. Thick set, around five feet eight or nine. Dark, even swarthy, with a very definite accent.' The Battle of Britain veteran pursed his lips. 'A rather dubious character, Mr Temple, if you ask me.'

'Had you ever seen him before?' Paul asked. 'I mean, before this morning when he called with the letter?'

'No. Clayton made the reservation here by phone. Then early this morning an American car pulled up in front of the hotel and Mr Clayton got out. He said he was very sorry he had to cancel his reservation, and would I be kind enough to hand this message to Mr Temple at eleven o'clock.'

'There must be a mistake somewhere,' said Paul.

The landlord raised an enquiring eyebrow.

'The Danny Clayton you describe doesn't sound like the Danny Clayton I came here to meet.'

'Is that a fact? It's a mystery, Mr Temple.'

'Very true,' said Paul. But the mystery of which was the real Danny Clayton was quickly solved. When Paul arrived back in London he found the real one waiting in his study.

Chapter Five

It was the Danny Clayton whom Margaret Milbourne had described. The young slim one in a hurry. He had been using a great deal of urgent charm on Steve, it appeared. They were in the kitchen together eating the remains of lunch and finishing a bottle of wine. Steve loved Switzerland and had a weakness for people who could talk about the country as though they lived there. Danny had lived there for more than three years.

'Darling, we thought you wouldn't be back for lunch,' Steve said lightly. 'We waited till nearly two, and then Danny and I were so hungry –'

Paul glared at the visitor. 'That's all right, I had a turkey sandwich. What are you doing here, Mr Clayton?'

'I came to see you. I'm Julia Carrington's secretary, and she asked me to come to London and consult you –'

'Did Miss Carrington give you my address, or did you get that from Mrs Milbourne?'

Danny Clayton laughed in a way that Paul found slightly offensive. 'I looked you up in the telephone directory,' he said, pushing away the cheese plate in a well-fed gesture.

'You do know Mrs Milbourne?' Paul persisted.

'Yes, of course. I've met the woman. She's mad. She telephoned me at my hotel just after I arrived from Geneva. I'm staying at the New Wilton and I was taking a shower after the journey when the telephone rang.' He lit a small cigar and sat back expansively. Somehow he managed to convey that the size of the cigar was a move away from vulgar excess. 'She wanted to meet me.'

'And out of the kindness of your heart,' Paul suggested, 'you agreed?'

'Yes, you could put it that way. The name Milbourne was familiar, and then I remembered that a publisher called Carl Milbourne had visited Julia a few weeks back. He got himself killed next day. So I agreed to see the damn woman. She was anxious, and I had a spare evening.'

Paul sat in the grandmother chair and settled down for a long story; at least this was something he could check. And so far it was wrong. Paul didn't quite take to the brash young man. Engaging, but obviously not entirely scrupulous.

'When Carl Milbourne visited Julia Carrington, did she see him?'

'No,' said Clayton. 'I saw him instead. That's the usual routine. Julia refuses to have anything to do with publishers or journalists, and it's my job to give them the brush-off.'

Steve interrupted to ask whether it was true that Julia Carrington had written her memoirs.

'No truth in it whatever, Mrs Temple. And that was what I told Carl Milbourne.' Danny grinned. 'I don't think Milbourne believed me. He thought I was trying to get rid of him. The interview wasn't exactly a pleasant one, I'm afraid. That was why I felt a trifle guilty the next day when I read about his accident.'

'What happened when Mrs Milbourne turned up at your hotel?' Paul asked. 'I suppose she did turn up?'

'Oh yes, she turned up all right. We had a weird conversation in the cocktail bar. She arrived looking like a neurotic Electra, chain smoking and radiating desperation. I can cope with women like that – I knew a lot of them in Hollywood.' He laughed. 'In fact, I suppose I work for a woman like that. Julia imagines that her life is a full-scale Greek tragedy.'

'Tell me about the weird conversation,' Paul murmured.

Danny Clayton had been confused. 'She insisted that her husband was still alive,' he said with a grin. 'But her reasoning wasn't up to much. She said she'd found proof in a hat that arrived through the post.'

'But why did she want to see you, Mr Clayton?'

'I don't know. I suppose I was one of the last people to see her husband before he died. If he died. But I couldn't help her to find the guy, and she wasn't very coherent.'

'Mrs Milbourne has been upset since she came back from Switzerland,' Steve explained to him. 'Her brother is worried about her.'

'Boy, he has my sympathy,' said Clayton. 'He has a real problem on his hands.'

Paul poured himself some coffee before he spoke. He watched the American and tried to decide whether he was telling the truth. 'Mr Clayton,' he said eventually, 'I'd better be frank with you. Mrs Milbourne gave me a very different version of her interview with you. She said it was you who told her that her husband was still alive. She said you showed her some photographs of Carl Milbourne, and that you offered the photographs and additional information for the price of five thousand pounds.'

Danny Clayton's thin features narrowed in astonishment. 'My God, that woman really is crazy!'

'She said you asked her to take the money to a hotel near Maidenhead. The Three Star Hotel at Bray-on-Thames.' Paul leaned across the table. 'Did you go down to Bray-on-Thames this morning, Mr Clayton?'

'I was in my hotel until eleven o'clock,' he said defensively. 'You can check that with the desk clerk.'

Paul was still sceptical. 'So I take it you've never heard of a man called Peter Fletcher, or the houseboat he lived on called Peter's Folly?'

'That's right, I haven't.' He stubbed out the cigar and turned to face Paul with a youthful frankness. 'This is only my second visit to England, so I don't know many people and I never heard of Maidenhead or the other place you mentioned. I promise you, Mr Temple, the only reason I'm over here is to see you.'

'Ah yes,' Paul said ironically, 'you were going to consult me.'

Clayton rose to his feet looking pained. 'That's right, I was.'

'Well?'

He walked irritably across to the window and stared into the mews, then he visibly regained his composure. 'Julia Carrington has been receiving unpleasant letters, Mr Temple, letters threatening blackmail. She needs your help.'

'What is in these letters?'

'I don't know.' He returned to the table. 'I haven't seen them, but I gather they're unpleasant. They've certainly frightened poor Julia.'

'Has she consulted the police?'

'Gee no!' he said earnestly. 'That's the last thing she would do. If Julia consulted the police that would mean the newspapers, journalists and the lot! Why do you think she retired to Switzerland? You only have to mention publicity for Julia to go berserk. She had enough of that in Hollywood.'

'All right,' said Paul. He stood up to indicate that the discussion was over. 'When are you returning to Geneva?'

'The day after tomorrow.' Clayton was unsure of himself, as if he were aware that the youthful brashness didn't charm Temple. 'I took the liberty of making reservations for you and Mrs Temple on the same flight. Everything's taken care of. All you have to do is say that you'll help.'

'American efficiency,' Steve intruded quickly. 'You inspire confidence, Mr Clayton.'

Paul accepted defeat with a sigh. 'All right, we'll come out with you, Mr Clayton. Even if we fly back on the next plane.' He shrugged. 'I've been wanting to have a chat with Miss Carrington anyway. I've recently been hearing so much about her.'

'From whom?' Danny Clayton asked as he put on a mink-lined overcoat.

'From a film director friend of mine called Vince Langham. I understand you recently threw him out on his ear as well.'

Clayton laughed. 'I wouldn't put it as bluntly as that. But he had a novel he was crazy about and he wanted Julia to star in the film version. We get these approaches all the time.'

'Did either you or Miss Carrington read the novel?'

'Julia retired, Mr Temple, she doesn't want to go back into the crazy world of films. So there's no reason for her or me to read any of these scripts.' He threw out his hands in a gesture of apology. 'I hope I wasn't too rough on your friend.'

'Vince has a pretty thick skin.'

'Well, it's been nice talking to you, Mr Temple.' He shook hands and thanked Steve for the lunch. His charm was still working for Steve.

'Did you believe his version of the encounter with Margaret Milbourne?' Paul asked her.

Steve smiled. 'I found him rather persuasive,' she said ambiguously.

Yes, Paul reflected, the fellow was a hustler. He had been a success in Hollywood, arriving there at the age of nineteen and scrambling to the top in the front offices, surviving palace revolutions, the reforms imposed by New York bankers and the conversion of the studios to full-scale television production. Danny Clayton's power of persuasion had enabled him to survive and prosper. It was uncharacteristic of him to have thrown away his career when Julia retired.

'So we're going to Switzerland after all,' said Steve.

'So it would seem. I'd better find myself some holiday reading.'

Paul knew the fiction editor of Milbourne & Co. so he popped into the man's office on his way to see Vince Langham. The pall of tragedy on the house was hardly noticeable. Milbourne & Co. was an old-fashioned firm which didn't believe in excitement or salesmanship, and every day was like the day of a funeral. The men all wore city suits and spoke in hushed tones; the girls were discreetly attractive.

'Temple, this is a pleasant surprise!' said Norman Wallace. 'Come in and have a cup of tea. Have you decided to get yourself a good publisher at last?'

Paul chatted for a few minutes about the world of books, who had been sacked and which was the latest masterpiece that would rock the world. The gossip was not something that Paul enjoyed, but he had to get Wallace on to the subject of new writers.

'Ah yes,' Wallace said regretfully, 'Carl and I were just forming a bunch of really promising new writers.'

'You mean people like Richard Randolph.'

'And one or two others,' Norman Wallace said loyally. 'But Randolph was Carl's own private discovery. Carl had great hopes that *Too Young to Die* would be a real winner. Do you know that we've already sold the film rights for fifty thousand dollars?'

'Yes,' said Paul as he mentally halved the figure and converted it to sterling. 'Do you happen to have a spare copy of the book?'

Norman Wallace produced a copy on condition that Paul said something they could quote in the publicity. 'A rattling good yarn from start to finish: I couldn't put it down.' Something that would sell it to the middle-class housewives with time on their hands. Wallace took a list from his left-hand drawer and was adding Paul's name to it.

'Is that the distribution list for advance copies?' Paul asked casually. 'I've always wondered how you choose the names to go on there. For instance, why should Peter Fletcher receive a copy?'

Norman Wallace read solemnly through the list. 'He didn't. Although the name sounds familiar. Isn't he mentioned in the afternoon paper?' A copy of the *Evening News* was in his filing tray. '*Houseboat Murder near Maidenhead. Artist Found Stabbed*'. Norman Wallace became more cautious. 'Is that why you're here, Paul? Are you investigating a murder?'

'Well, yes, but not that particular murder. Incidentally, why isn't Vince Langham's name on your list?'

Norman Wallace read through the list again. 'You're quite right, it's been left off. Langham phoned yesterday and we sent a copy round to his flat.' He added the name in an illegible scrawl. 'Although he read the book many months ago. In typescript, I suppose.'

Norman Wallace sat back and stared unhappily at the ceiling. 'I was trying to persuade Carl to get some of Langham's film scripts for publication. He's a brilliant writer and I'm sure they would create the right kind of stir.'

'I'll mention it to Vince,' said Paul. 'I'm just off to see him.'

Somebody poked a bald head round the door and called, 'Coming for a drink, Norman? Half past five. I said I'd meet –' He broke off and advanced into the room with a friendly hand outstretched. 'Hello, is this a spy from the enemy camp? Come on, Temple, join us for a quick half pint.'

A quick half pint with Ben Sainsbury could amount to a punishing evening: a battered ego and a hangover. But it was the best way to find out how Milbourne & Co. were surviving. Ben Sainsbury was the other half of the editorial team, in charge of non-fiction. He was totally different from Wallace, which was probably why they worked together so well. Ben was extrovert, aggressive and opinionated, chubby and indiscreet. Not a gentleman.

'Love to,' said Paul with cautious enthusiasm.

Ben had gone into publishing from journalism after writing a single, sensitive novel, which nobody ever mentioned in his presence. Ben didn't like it to be thought that beneath the bluff exterior there was a sensitive soul asking to be left alone. He hunched inside his overcoat and talked all the way to the pub about the iniquities of the government.

It was a pretentious pub with lots of brass bedpans and wooden gargoyles, intimate partitioning and a landlord like a retired colonel. 'I hate this place,' said Ben, looking distantly at the pub on the other side of the road, 'but it is the nearest.' He borrowed a fiver from Norman Wallace and then generously bought drinks for the three of them.

'Careful,' he whispered to Wallace. 'There's Jameson over there.' He turned conspiratorially to Paul. 'He's our accountant. An informer.'

Wallace looked faintly embarrassed and sipped his light ale. 'He was telling me this afternoon that he's thinking of leaving. There's a job going with –'

'Lies, he was trying to lull you into a false sense of security, so that you would leave. Do you know, the other evening he spent two hours with me, analysing what was wrong with the firm. Of course, I nodded from time to time out of sheer politeness, and he went back to Carl and repeated every word I said. Carl was terribly hurt.'

'The other evening?' Paul asked in surprise.

'Yes, just after I'd come back from my summer holidays. Jameson had been busy. We nearly sold out to a bloody American airline. He's a bloody accountant! What do we want with accountants in publishing?'

'To keep an eye on your expense account,' Wallace said with a laugh. He looked at his watch. 'Oh well, six o'clock, I must be off.' He shook hands with Paul and said how pleasant to see him again. 'See you tomorrow, Ben.'

Ben was ordering more doubles at the bar, but he waved. 'Norman lives in Wembley, in a semi. He has a wife. Have you ever been to Wembley?'

'Well yes, actually,' Paul confessed.

'We do our best to keep Norman on the straight and narrow, but he has to be watched. He has secret yearnings to spend his Sunday mornings in the garden polishing the plastic gnomes.'

'You can buy special wet-look gnomes,' said Paul, 'they don't need polishing. Just a wash down with the garden hose.'

'What a missed opportunity – I bought Norman a book for Christmas. He would have much preferred a wet-look gnome.'

Paul invested in three rounds of drinks before eight o'clock; they were repeatedly interrupted by Ben's competitors and colleagues, name-droppers and grandiose talk about deals, but it was useful, especially when Paul asked directly what Carl Milbourne had been like.

'To work for? Well, he couldn't read, but I suppose that's an advantage in publishing. He started the firm with his army annuity after the war, and he did quite well, don't you think? All this, built on four hundred pounds. His early days were a struggle. He only really made the first division when he happened on a series of escape stories and second world war adventure yarns. That was when Norman and I joined him and turned Milbourne & Co. into a publishing firm.'

'So he wasn't really a businessman,' said Paul.

'This isn't really a business,' said Ben. 'He was a dilettante. Very clever, but he preferred the social life. That was how the firm ran into trouble.'

'During the summer,' Paul murmured.

'That's right. He started to dabble in business. He sacked our old inefficient accountant who always balanced the books so that we made a profit and he brought in Jameson. Well, I mean, as long as you make a profit what does it matter? We were all doing very nicely, with big dividends and salaries and the books were selling. But Jameson had to prove himself.'

Ben ordered another large gin and another small whisky in some distress. 'Cheers. Henry bloody Jameson changed the method of accounting and showed that we had been losing money for years. When he produced his figures for the last financial year we were almost bankrupt!'

'What did you do?' asked Paul.

'Well, I thought there was only one thing to do, and that was to sack Jameson. But Carl had no head for business – he took one look at the balance sheets and he panicked. One week he tried to streamline the firm by sacking the publicity head and getting in a whizz-bang girl straight from art school, next week he wanted to sell out to an American airline. He didn't know what to do.'

Paul laughed. 'And what,' he asked, 'did Carl do eventually?'

'I don't know. I suppose he pulled himself together and forgot about it. Norman and I promised to cut down on our expense accounts and he went off to Switzerland a happy man.' He sighed and stared significantly at his empty glass. 'If it hadn't been for Jameson he'd have still been alive today.'

'What do you mean?'

'Carl would never have chased off to secure a film star's memoirs, he'd have left it to me and I wouldn't have bothered. We have film stars' memoirs coming into the office from our American branch every day, and most of them are rubbish. I'd want to see what Julia Carrington had written before I'd go out to Switzerland. I'd want to know whether the Sunday papers would buy the serial rights. Carl went flying off to his death on a bloody whim.'

'It must have been a blow to you.'

'I suppose it doesn't make any difference. Norman and I are still running the firm as we always did. But it was rather unnecessary, that's all.'

'What are you going to do now?' Paul asked.

'Sack the whizz-bang girl from art school, if Margaret Milbourne will let us,' he said savagely. 'Or do you mean tonight? I'm staying here. I said I'd meet a literary agent here around nine o'clock. . .'

Paul left him talking to a proof-reader on the other side of the bar. There was a fog gathering outside so Paul buttoned up his overcoat and hailed a taxi.

Vince Langham lived the life of a travelling showman; his Knightsbridge home was expensive, but it looked as if he were in the process of either moving in or moving out, and it had looked like that for the past sixteen years. Vince claimed that whenever he had a few months between films he tried to make it a home, but then he had to fly off on location, raise money or go on holiday. Vince was surrounded by packing cases, half-laid carpets and paintings waiting to be hung. He was sitting in the middle of the floor eating fish fingers, drinking whisky and listening to a Linguaphone course.

'Hi,' he called as Paul was shown in by Mrs Langham. 'Have you eaten this evening, or can Sarah throw some more fish fingers in the pan?'

'I told Steve I'd be back for dinner,' said Paul. 'She insisted that you would be too busy cutting and editing your new film.'

'It's the old film now. Somebody else does the cutting and editing. The studio janitor, as Orson would say. They think if they didn't take all the cans away from me now the result might be art. So I'm working on my next project. If you chuck that tape recorder on the floor you should find an armchair underneath it.'

Paul sat amid the clutter and poured himself some whisky. 'What's the new project?' he asked.

'I don't know. I was thinking on the way back from Victoria Station about Julia Carrington. You set the whole thing going again in my mind. I thought maybe I'd go to Switzerland and have another crack at her.'

'*Ich stand an einer Strassenecke. Sie nannten es Einbruch*,' declaimed the record player.

'Americans have a bad name for not bothering to learn the lingo,' said Vince. 'I thought I'd make an effort. I'm not going till Friday.'

Paul laughed. 'I wondered why you had asked Norman Wallace for another copy of *Too Young to Die*. I suppose you lost your original copy?'

Vince joined in the laughter. 'I've lost the new copy as well. I'm hoping Sarah will clear this place through for me while I'm away.' They both looked through at Sarah in the kitchen and realised it was improbable. She had been an actress, and she bent over the sink like Marlene Dietrich waiting for the director to call 'Cut'. She was a star. 'I hired a charwoman a few months ago,' said Vince. 'She was nearly sixty and her voice was so cockney I couldn't understand a word she said. But do you know she only came to me because she wanted to break into films?'

It was the same with being a novelist; Paul sometimes wondered whether he would ever fall into casual conversation with anybody who had not written a novel. The Linguaphone record ground on and then repeated itself, the whisky grew lower in the bottle and the evening passed. At ten o'clock, as Paul was about to leave, Vince Langham looked suddenly suspicious.

'By the way, Paul, why did you come to see me this evening?'

Paul laughed. 'I came to find out where your copies of *Too Young to Die* had got to. But you told me that some time ago. You said you lost them.'

Vince relaxed. 'I lose everything, and it always looks bad on my record. What does it prove this time?'

'It doesn't prove anything. But it means that your copy of the book might have been on Peter Fletcher's houseboat this morning.'

'What, in Bray-on-Thames?'

'That's right. You were one of the two people who knew that I was going out to Bray this morning.'

Vince nodded solemnly. 'To see Danny Clayton. I remember.'

'Well, don't sit there agreeing with me. Tell me that you've never heard of Peter Fletcher, that you were in bed at half past ten this morning. Come on, Vince, say something.'

Vince Langham looked pained and rose to his feet. 'Temple, you tried to trick me there. You know perfectly well that I once worked with Peter Fletcher. I don't think that was nice, it wasn't British, after drinking so much of my whisky. Especially since on television tonight it said that he'd been bumped off.'

'You worked with him a long time ago,' Paul said lamely. 'I thought you might have forgotten.'

'He was a brilliant designer. Shallow as hell, of course, but he achieved exactly the effects I wanted, and that's what I call genius.' He laughed and punched Paul on the arm. 'I always remember genius. I remember you, don't I, from all that time ago when we worked together?'

It was such a nice remark that Paul decided to leave for home. Why spoil a nice compliment?

'Is Tully about?'

The manager stared at something past Paul's right shoulder. 'No. And I've never heard of anybody called Tully. Who wants him?'

'Tell him Paul Temple needs some advice.'

The manager's gaze flickered across Paul's face and settled on to his left shoulder. 'Wait here, Mr Temple.'

He disappeared into Tully's fun palace leaving Paul by the gymnastic display of photographs in the foyer. This had been a flourishing gambling club until Tully lost his licence under the 1968 Gaming Act, and now it was a night club. The advertisements proclaimed the hottest floor show in Soho.

'This way, Mr Temple.'

The manager led him through a baize door and upstairs through the dressing rooms and offices to Tully's personal suite. They passed numerous bored-looking girls resting between performances and a number of tough-looking bouncers. The atmosphere was decidedly menacing, which was appropriate to Tully's taste for the dramatic.

'Temple! Good to see you again. What is your wife thinking of to let you out at this time of night?'

Tully was loud and extrovert with a cockney accent. He was in his fifties but he didn't yet look as if he needed all those bouncers to protect him. He went across to the cocktail cabinet and poured two large brandies.

'I see from the papers you had an accident with your car,' he said with a roar of laughter. 'I hope you don't think any of my boys would –'

'No no, Tully, I know all your boys are law-abiding citizens. I'm here about one of the girls you employ.'

Tully stood thoughtfully in front of a blazing coal fire and warmed his bottom. 'Ah yes, Dolly Brazier. Poor kid.'

'You know what happened to her?' Paul asked in surprise.

'My manager told me she was beaten up.'

'But you employ a hundred people, Tully. How did you guess I was here to ask about Dolly?'

He finished his brandy and put the empty glass on the mantelshelf before replying. 'I know she's a friend of yours, that's how. We had a long chat about you a few weeks ago, when the producer threw her out of the Amazon chorus and I was supposed to sack her.' Tully smiled. 'For old times' sake, I didn't sack her. She has quite a crush on you, Paul.'

'Do you know who attacked her?'

'Not yet, but two of my boys are looking into the matter.' It sounded dire. 'I don't approve of people who use violence on women. Or at least, not on my women.'

His moral earnestness almost made Paul grin. 'She was told to warn me off a case, which she did. I suppose the violence was to make sure she doesn't reveal who put her up to it.'

'She obviously talks too much about her friendship with you, Temple.'

There was a buzz at the door. 'I expect this will be my boys,' said Tully. They were middle-aged boys with impassive faces and bulky clothes. They radiated suspicion as they shook hands with Paul.

'Any luck?' asked Tully.

'Well, she lives in Kilburn, you see, chief. He was waiting for her to come out. That was how it happened.'

'He? Who did it?'

'She was done over by Mickey Stone and his side-kick,' said one of them. 'It was a cash job.'

'Did you find out who hired him?' asked Tully.

'No chance, chief, you can't intimidate Mickey Stone. But I tell you, he'll be out of action for a few months.'

The two impassive faces broke into happy smiles.

'I don't like you going to see Tully by yourself,' said Steve. 'I know about those girls he has working at the dub.'

'I thought it would save time if I went by myself, darling; surely you wouldn't have wanted to come?'

'No, but you could have taken Kate as a chaperone.'

'She looks like an ex-policewoman. The girls would have taken one look at her and started to sing Gilbert and Sullivan fully clothed.'

'What's wrong with a few clothes?' She smiled severely. 'I wear clothes myself and make quite a striking impression.' She turned out the light beside the bed. 'Or do you think that I'm dull?'

'Certainly not, darling. None of the girls who work for Tully have a tenth of your intellect.' Paul climbed into bed.

'I hate you.'

Chapter Six

The air terminal was thronged with impatient people complaining vigorously of the London fog, but they made no difference. All planes were grounded. Paul Temple searched through the crowds for nearly ten minutes in search of Danny Clayton, and eventually he found Clayton in a telephone kiosk putting through a call to Geneva.

'Just telling Julia we shan't be going,' he explained. 'She insists that it's my fault there's a fog, but I told her that England will not be moved. When the continent is cut off it's cut off.'

'The trains are still running, and so is the ferry from Dover,' said Paul. 'I've used a little influence with an old friend of mine and I've managed to get three sleepers on the two thirty train from Victoria. We'll be in Geneva tomorrow morning about ten o'clock.'

Danny Clayton clapped his hands with boyish delight. 'I hadn't thought of that! We can go by train, it'll be much more fun. I always hate flying anyway.'

They carried their suitcases the hundred yards or so along to Victoria Station, past people with handkerchiefs clutched nervously to their faces, finding their way among the yellow lights which loomed at them from shops and cars. It was rather pleasant, Paul reflected, like the London of his boyhood before pea-soupers were abolished. He liked the slightly sooty smell. The noise of footsteps and distant voices was strangely clear in the fog.

'I've just remembered,' said Danny Clayton, 'I hate travelling by boat as well. I'm always seasick.'

'It only takes an hour and a half to cross the channel,' Steve said reassuringly.

A porter found them and took their suitcases away to the luggage compartment while another showed them to the train and found their compartment. The train was filled with people who had had the same idea, talking nostalgically of the days before they flew everywhere. Travelling by rail seemed so much more natural.

'If God had meant us to fly,' an elderly gentleman was saying, 'He'd have given us wings.'

The train drew out of the station. Paul took out that morning's *Times* and began doing the crossword. Steve closed her eyes and began dozing. Danny Clayton talked all the way to Dover. To each his own style of travel.

They passed quickly through customs and went aboard the channel ferry to find their cabins. Almost immediately the engine shuddered and they were off. Danny Clayton turned pale.

'Why don't you come up on deck, Danny?' asked Paul. 'The breeze and a spot of exercise may help.'

Danny sank on to the bunk. 'I'm pretty comfortable like this,' he said gingerly. 'I guess I'll stay down here.'

'How about you, Steve?'

'I'd like a stroll, darling, if Danny will be all right.' She turned to him anxiously. 'Are you sure you wouldn't like to go down to the bar for a drink? A brandy –?'

'I'll be all right,' he said.

Paul took Steve's arm and they went up on deck. They took the ritual walk round the perimeter rail and breathed the air until Paul felt that his lungs were in danger. As they reached the starboard bow they saw Maurice Lonsdale disappearing down the staircase.

'What's he doing here?' asked Paul in surprise.

'We could ask him,' said Steve. 'I expect he's gone down to the bar.'

'That's an excellent excuse for a drink,' Paul laughed.

But Lonsdale had vanished. The bar was filled with people buying duty free drinks. Paul wondered whether he had been mistaken about Lonsdale, perhaps it had been another millionaire trying to protect his cigar from the sea spray.

They ordered two brandies and sat watching the horizon dip and sway through the porthole. You're closer to eternity at sea, thought Paul, closer to God. Although for philosophic reflections one really ought to be in the middle of the Indian ocean at night. Crossing the channel was a little mundane.

'I wonder how Danny is taking this weather,' said Steve.

'I was thinking deep thoughts about Freud and his oceanic theory.'

'The proper place for Freud, darling, is in bed. Oh look, here comes Danny now!'

'What on earth has happened to him?' Paul muttered.

He was looking very sick indeed. His sallow complexion had a sheen of damp that reflected the light and the long hair seemed matted and unhealthy. He saw them, waved, and pushed across the floor towards them.

'Try to hang on,' Paul said reassuringly. 'We'll be docking in about twenty-five minutes.'

Danny tried to smile and glanced nervously around the room at the same time. 'I felt like a breath of fresh air, but when I got on deck the boat started to roll . . .' He flopped into the seat facing the door.

'You look as if you've had a scare of some kind,' said Steve. 'Why not let Paul fetch you a brandy?'

'A scare?' he repeated anxiously. 'No no, I'm always like this when I travel.'

Paul Temple fetched him a brandy and then made excuses about seeing to the hand luggage while Steve played Florence Nightingale.

He went back to the cabin. He found a steward in the corridor and asked him whether Danny Clayton had received any visitors while he was lying down.

'Not to my knowledge, sir,' said the steward. 'But I've been back and forth, I might not have seen everybody who came down here.'

'I say, if it isn't Paul Temple,' said a man in a bowler hat from the next cabin. 'I don't suppose you'll remember me. We were on television together once, some damned chat show about crime being a bad thing. Have you solved any good mysteries lately?'

Paul shook hands with the man and tried to remember his name. He had been in Military Intelligence, or perhaps he was retired. Paul said something non-committal about bad weather for spying.

'Are you trying to find out what scared the pants off your little friend?' the man asked.

'Not really, just wondering whether –'

'Nonsense, somebody scared the pants off him. I was behind him when we went up on deck. He was pretty fragile, but then he obviously saw something that went beyond *mal*

74

de mer. If I didn't weigh fifteen stone he'd have knocked me down those stairs, he was so anxious to escape! Going skiing?'

'No. I'm visiting friends in Geneva.'

'You'll be much safer,' the man said solemnly. 'I'm popping into the Palais des Nations. Maybe we'll have a drink together.' He glanced out of the porthole. 'Ah well, another sea trip safely negotiated. Your friend should be all right now.' He waved his rolled umbrella in salute. 'What I always say is that if you're still alive you haven't much to complain about.'

'Very true,' murmured Paul.

Going through customs at Calais was a ritual that was quickly over, and as they crossed the dock to the waiting train Paul caught another glimpse of Maurice Lonsdale. Danny Clayton recovered from his sea sickness or his scare as soon as they were seated in the railway carriage. He began chattering again while Steve dozed and Paul wondered what information was essential to the brinkman with nine letters.

'I suppose you play chess as well,' said Danny.

'Yes,' said Paul. 'Do you?'

'No. I just thought it all tied in with your being a private eye. I prefer easy games like Monopoly. Ask me one of your crossword clues.'

'What information is essential to the brinkman? Nine letters.'

Steve opened one eye. 'Knowledge.'

'Gosh,' said Danny. 'I didn't know you were brilliant as well, Steve.'

Paul scowled at her and wrote in the answer.

'How long have you been over here, Danny?' Steve asked.

'In Europe? Four years.'

'Do you prefer it to America?'

He laughed. 'It's different. I do feel homesick sometimes, but I don't suppose Julia will ever go back. She's found a tiny world where she can hide, and I'll stay with her while she remains in hiding. She couldn't bear the real life of America. That's probably why she became an actress.'

'I'm not sure what you mean by the real life of America,' said Paul, 'but I'd have thought you were a natural for the pace and the competition.'

'I carry it inside me. I don't need to go to New York to find it.'

Danny talked about his childhood in the Bronx for a while, and about his father selling automobiles in the depressed 'thirties. When the boom years began again after the war Danny's family had moved out to California.

'Are your parents still out there?' Paul asked.

'No, both my folks are dead. They lost their lives in a fire – a large apartment house in Los Angeles was razed to the ground. It was in all the papers. Two of the old movie stars were killed as well. About twenty seven people lost their lives altogether.'

'What a terrible thing,' Paul murmured.

'Were you away at the time?' Steve asked.

'No, I was in the fire. I was caught too. Fortunately I was in the basement at the time, talking to a friend of mine. I was one of the lucky ones.'

As the afternoon wore on the train passed through wine-growing country, and Paul watched the undulating miles of vineyards with a feeling of loss for the holiday he had spent picking grapes during his student years. Long before he met Steve. He was on the point of mentioning it when he remembered a dark-haired French girl called – what had her name been? He decided not to mention the holiday.

'Darling,' said Steve, 'isn't this where you picked grapes the year before we met?'

He peered through the window. 'Good lord, I do believe it is! I'd completely forgotten –'

'You had an affair with a redhead called Hélène.'

'Hélène? Yes, I seem to remember there was a girl on the camp with auburn hair.'

'You had her photograph on your dressing table the first time I came to dinner and I was terribly jealous. So I gave you a photograph of me instead.' Steve leaned her head on his shoulder. 'I didn't think she was very attractive. Too much flesh, and a sulky expression.'

'She helped me improve my French,' said Paul. 'We used to have long conversations about the pen of her aunt.'

'Liar.'

Paul took his copy of *Too Young to Die* from the luggage rack and tried to read. The opening sentence didn't inspire much confidence. *There is no such place as Hollywood; Hollywood is an idea, a way of life and a way to die.* It was one of those stories about an actress who arrives as an innocent and learns corruption. By *Sunset Boulevard* out of *The Big Knife*.

Why did Norman Wallace think this was the work of a promising young writer? There was no resonance to the writing; it was all dialogue and fragmentary scenes, the prose was cluttered with phrases like 'In so far as blah blah blah was concerned' and 'with reference to' and on page two somebody riposted. Paul didn't like the description of the heroine's leading men; they ranged from Gable types to aspiring James Deans, whatever range that was. By page twenty she was in bed with one of them.

Paul found that his attention was straying. The countryside had become dramatically rugged with snow-covered hills in the distance; a river reflected the sun like a sliver of silver.

There were farms dotted about with neat little fences and neat farmhouses.

'I spent a holiday on a farm once,' said Steve. 'I was nine and the farmer's son taught me to milk a cow.'

'Last time you told me about that holiday,' said Paul, 'it was an anecdote about watching a calf being born. It was all rather Emile Zola and quite unsuitable for a girl of nine.'

'Darling, I do believe you're sulking.'

'Just bored.' He tossed the book on to the seat beside him. 'I find actresses rather unconvincing as people.'

'Hey,' Danny Clayton interrupted, 'that's an epigram. I must remember to say that to Julia one day when I'm mad at her.' He picked up the book and began reading it.

After dinner on the train they felt suddenly tired and went in search of their sleeping berths. That was when Paul at last bumped into a startled Maurice Lonsdale.

'I thought I saw you earlier,' Paul said. 'What an exercise in nostalgia, eh? Travelling across Europe like this.'

'Yes, so much for the jet age!' He beamed at Steve. 'Hello, Mrs Temple. Delighted to meet you again.'

Steve smiled sweetly and went on with Danny Clayton to the sleeping cars while Paul talked to Lonsdale. 'What brings you out here so suddenly, Lonsdale? You didn't mention –'

'An accident, I'm afraid. Friend of mine out here for a skiing holiday has broken her leg. Freda Sands, I think I mentioned her. She isn't terribly clever at coping with hospitals and being confined to bed.' He laughed bluffly. 'Poor Freda. She's only been to St Moritz once before and that time she broke her arm.'

'I thought the train for St Moritz went via Zurich,' said Paul, 'changing at Chur. This is the train to Lausanne and Geneva.'

78

Lonsdale looked taken aback. 'Yes yes, I believe you're right. But I have some business in Geneva. Might as well kill two birds in one trip, as they say. My goodness, is that the time?' He muttered apologetically about the change of air making one so tired and then continued along the corridor.

'See you tomorrow, I expect,' Paul called after him.

Steve was already in her bunk and settled for sleep by the time Paul had finished his preparations for bed. Paul spent several minutes searching for his copy of *Too Young* to *Die* but it was missing.

'I expect Danny borrowed it,' said Steve. 'You'll just have to go to sleep.'

The rhythmic motion of the train made it easy to sleep. Paul could hear Steve's regular breathing on the other side of the carriage and he wondered irrationally at the sheer green nylon nightdress: it would be such unsuitable wear if they crashed.

'Do you suppose it was Lonsdale who scared poor Danny?' she whispered.

'I thought you were asleep.'

'Did you get the impression just now that they knew each other?' she asked.

'They weren't letting on if they did,' said Paul.

He was wearing suitable silk pyjamas that would look correct in any situation, which was useful a few hours later when Steve woke him up to say that something was going on in the next compartment.

'It sounds as if Danny has been hurt,' she said.

Paul listened. There was certainly a lot of movement and moaning.

'I'm not sure what woke me,' said Steve. 'I think it was somebody shouting, and I heard a door slam.'

'Are you certain?'

'No, but I think so. I was asleep and it woke me.'

Paul swung himself out of the bunk and snatched his dressing gown. There was nobody in the corridor. The lights were dimmed and the train was hurtling through the darkness. Paul knocked on Danny Clayton's door.

'Danny!' He knocked again. 'Are you all right?'

Danny's voice answered weakly. 'What is it?'

'Are you all right in there?'

'Yeah, fine,' he answered. But the door remained closed. 'I fell out of my bunk, that's all. Sorry if I disturbed you.'

In the morning Danny had a bruised cheek and from the way he winced as he sat down to breakfast it seemed as if his body was badly bruised. So somebody had given him a second warning, thought Paul. He couldn't quite see Lonsdale as a strong-arm man, although Danny was a frail enough character. The streets of New York would have taught Danny to use his wits rather than his fists.

'I was climbing into bed when the train gave one of those Goddammed lurches. My suitcase fell on top of me.'

'Your face looks painful,' murmured Paul.

'That's why I hate travelling by train,' he said with a grin.

It was half past eight. Paul was drinking his second cup of coffee, Danny was drinking a tomato juice and Steve was eating her way through a hearty meal as the train drew into Lausanne.

'This,' said Paul, 'is where we change.'

Chapter Seven

The Geneva train arrived at the Gare de Cornovin at half past ten. Paul and Steve went directly to their hotel in the Rue du Mont Blanc. They had arranged that Danny would collect them at half past six for dinner with Julia Carrington, so they had eight hours in which to explore one of Paul's favourite cities and visit Walter Neider.

'It's a swizz,' said Steve as she tossed her handbag on to the bed. 'We can't see Mont Blanc from the window.'

'We could on a clear day,' said Paul, 'if the window were facing east.' He looked on to the charming narrow streets rising up the hillside and decided that he preferred this direction. It was less intimidating than a range of mountains.

'I think I'll take a look at Geneva while you're with Mr Neider,' said Steve. 'A spot of sightseeing will make this seem like a holiday.'

Neider was an important man and it had required influence to reach him. Sir Graham Forbes had arranged it. Neider's office was a dark panelled hexagonal turret. He had a dramatic view of Lake Geneva from the windows which Paul found almost as awe-inspiring as the man himself.

'I hope you had a pleasant journey, Mr Temple. I gather the weather is dreadful in the north.'

Walter Neider probably weighed at least eighteen stone, yet his manner was impassioned. He lacked the phlegm which Paul expected of the Swiss. In moments of stress his language switched chaotically through French into German, Italian and English.

'Sir Graham told me you were interested in the Milbourne accident, Mr Temple.'

Paul sat by the window and nodded.

'So what can I do to help?'

'I'd like to hear your version of the accident,' Paul said. 'What exactly happened, Mr Neider?'

'It's quite simple. Carl Milbourne stepped off the pavement without looking, and he was knocked down by a car. It was not, I assure you, the fault of the driver; the man was completely exonerated.'

'Was there any doubt about the dead man's identity?' Paul asked.

'None whatsoever.' Neider looked surprised at the question. 'He was badly mangled, of course. The car dragged him some considerable distance. But he was wearing Carl Milbourne's clothes, he had letters, documents on him. They established his identity beyond any doubt.' He smiled, as if he suspected that Paul was trying to complicate a simple matter. 'Besides, Mrs Milbourne and her brother, a Mr Lonsdale, flew out here and identified the body.'

'Mrs Milbourne has since changed her mind.'

Neider spread his arms wide in incomprehension.

'She's now convinced that it wasn't her husband who was killed.'

'She was distressed,' said Neider. 'A bereaved woman can

82

be forgiven for such delusions. I assume you do not take her seriously?'

'I don't know yet,' said Paul. 'Some very odd things have been happening since she consulted me. Somebody was very keen that I shouldn't make any enquiries, and the same person has tried to prevent people from talking to me. I have a feeling –'

'What about evidence? Is there any evidence that Carl Milbourne might still be alive?'

'Maybe,' said Paul. 'Apparently he bought a hat from a shop in St Moritz. His old one was posted back to London; inside the lining of the hat was a note. It was in Carl Milbourne's handwriting and was written two days after the accident.'

Neider walked quickly round his desk. 'What did the note say, Mr Temple?'

'Briefly it said, *"Don't worry – everything will be all right. Will contact you later."* It isn't much to go on.'

'I take it you are going to St Moritz to question the people in the hat shop?'

'Eventually,' said Paul. 'But I have another reason for being in Geneva. Julia Carrington wants to see me.'

Neider looked impressed. 'Miss Carrington? Surely she has no interest in the Milbourne affair?'

'I hope not. Do you know Julia Carrington, Mr Neider?'

'Everyone knows Julia Carrington.' Which wasn't quite true. Neider confessed that like nearly everyone else, he knew of her. 'Actually I've only seen the lady once. She keeps herself very much to herself.'

'When did you see her?' asked Paul. 'Recently?'

'On January the fifth.'

Paul was surprised at the accuracy, the precision of the man's memory. But it turned out to be the date of Mrs Neider's birthday, as well as the day after the accident.

'I took my wife out to dinner, to a restaurant near Vevey,' he said thoughtfully. 'Miss Carrington was at the next table with her secretary, Danny Clayton. They were both in very high spirits – especially Miss Carrington. It was almost as if they were celebrating something.'

As Paul was leaving another question occurred to him. He paused as he was about to convey Sir Graham's best wishes for the new year. 'Neider, tell me: does the name Richard Randolph mean anything to you?'

'No, I don't think so.'

'He's an author,' said Paul, 'he's written a book called *Too Young to Die*. I believe it comes out some time next month.'

'I've never heard of him or the book. Should I have?'

'No,' said Paul. 'It's a very bad book. It isn't in the least important. Forget I asked.'

'I'm sure it is important, Mr Temple,' Neider said with a smile, 'or you wouldn't have asked. I'll remember the name.' He handed Paul his card and told him to drop in any time he needed help.

'You'll regret that invitation, Neider,' said Paul. 'I'll probably pester the life out of you.'

Well, at least that proved that the accident was probably genuine. Neider had been convinced. Paul walked towards the lake wishing that he had a staff to make those obvious checks that took so much time – checks on who inherited Carl Milbourne's estate and how much of it there was, and what would have happened if Milbourne had not been killed. Was he in debt? Come to think of it, Paul decided he didn't really know enough about Carl Milbourne.

The man's wife loved him, and he conducted a gentlemanly business. He was also sharp, clever and had married a fashionable actress. Lacking in dress sense and with a poor eye for prose. A finance firm would require a little more information before lending him money. What did the blighter do when he wasn't publishing books?

Steve was sitting on a seat near the bridge waiting for him, feeling restless and demanding a long walk to whet her appetite for lunch. Which suited Paul. He had a vague memory of an excellent restaurant on the other side of the lake.

It was half past one when they discovered the restaurant and Steve demanded a dry martini with the desperation of a not so bright young thing during the prohibition era. The restaurant was cosmopolitan and crowded with people. As Paul was wondering whether to order the *plat du jour* a film director came in.

'We might just as well have stayed in England,' said Paul. 'Everybody connected with this case has come to Geneva.'

'Good Lord,' said Steve, 'that's Vince Langham.'

Vince ambled across to join them. He embraced Steve as an old friend and sat at the table. 'Do you come here often?' he said cheerfully. 'This is my favourite restaurant. Have you seen the view?'

'You're disgustingly cheerful,' said Paul. 'Has Julia Carrington granted you an audience?'

'I'm seeing her tomorrow morning.'

'You are?' Paul said in surprise.

'I phoned her the moment I arrived and I was lucky enough to get the great lady herself. When I told her who I was she became pretty friendly. Quite different from that creep Danny Clayton.' He laughed proudly. 'She's giving me half an hour tomorrow morning.'

'Do you think you'll sell her the idea in half an hour?' Paul asked. 'I gather she isn't keen on making a come-back.'

'If I can persuade her to read the book, that's all it needs.' He turned to Paul. 'I found my copy of *Too Young to Die* in the drawer to my desk. It wasn't lost after all.'

'Oh well, if she doesn't want it perhaps you'll lend it to me,' said Paul. 'I lost my copy on the train.'

They ordered lunch and listened to Vince rehearsing his sales talk about *Too Young to Die;* he made it sound a more interesting book than the one Paul had begun. For one thing, Paul hadn't reached the part where she became a dipsomaniac.

'Were you on the train that reached Geneva at about ten this morning?' Paul asked. 'We didn't see you –'

'I stayed in my carriage, working on a film treatment,' said Vince. 'I always write my own scripts.'

'So Norman Wallace was saying.'

Vince Langham winced. 'Oh God, was he talking about publishing my film scripts again? They're only the damned words!'

The waiter arrived with the meal: pieces of lamb and bacon and a dish of haricot beans in sauce from the Danube; Steve sniffed ecstatically and quite lost interest in literature or crime. After all, as she said to Paul, this was supposed to be her holiday, remember?

'Dining with a brilliant film director I can accept,' she said with a grin at Vince. 'I don't mind dining with a famous American actress. But I refuse to spend my time worrying about clues.'

Julia Carrington lived in an isolated manor house thirty kilometres along the shore of Lake Geneva. It was less than twenty minutes along the wide motorway and another twenty minutes through the narrow mountain roads which brought them suddenly down to the lakeside once more. The manor house had four spires silhouetted against the night sky.

'I always say to Julia,' Danny Clayton observed ambiguously, 'that she lives like a film star. What do you think of all this?'

'Impressive,' Steve murmured.

They had been driven at high speed through the countryside by Danny, with headlamps dazzling across motorway and the wide expanse of snow, sometimes stabbing through empty blackness to a distant corner. It would have been safer, Paul was convinced, to keep the speed down to fifty; he would have had fewer bruises on his arm from Steve's tight grasp.

'How did you find Miss Carrington when you got home?' Paul asked him.

'She was in a curious mood,' Danny said over his shoulder. Paul wished he had kept silent. 'I asked her if she had received any more letters, but she refused to discuss the subject.'

'I wish you wouldn't keep turning round to look at me,' Paul said as they skidded round a bend.

'Before I left for London she was in a terrible state. That was why I came to see you. But now –' He changed gear and the car roared across a narrow bridge. 'She still seems worried, only more relaxed. Or perhaps more resigned, I don't know. Maybe she's a fatalist.'

The driveway seemed endless, and when eventually they drew up outside the house the massive doors were opened by a coloured manservant like Rochester. He ushered them into the hall and took their coats. There was a chandelier high above them, and expensive paintings faced them where the grand staircase in the centre forked and reached up to the balcony. Julia Carrington made her first appearance from a bedroom and came slowly down the staircase.

'How very nice to see you, Mr Temple. Mrs Temple. So good of you to come.' She was wearing a long white evening gown that trailed behind her. 'This is a pleasure,' she said as she reached the bottom stair and held out her hand, 'it really is. I've heard so many things about you.'

'Nice things, I hope?' murmured Paul.

'Always nice things. Let's go through into the drawing room. I hear you had quite an eventful journey.'

She was probably fifty, but she would have passed for thirty-five or even thirty in the artificial light. She had raven black hair and the figure of a girl. Only the faint lines on her neck and a tendency to crows' feet round her eyes made it seem possible that her first film had been made twenty seven years ago.

'There was fog in London,' said Paul. 'I think we'd all forgotten what it's like to cross Europe by train.'

'So I gather,' she said with a surprisingly throaty laugh. 'Suitcases falling in the night. Poor Danny looks like a featherweight boxer.'

Danny was at the tray pouring drinks. 'You don't understand, Julia, the sleepers are different over here. They aren't like the ones back home.'

'Silly boy,' she said mockingly. Julia Carrington bounced on to a chaise-longue and drew her legs up under her; the tomboy pose was in strange contrast to the grace with which she accepted her drink. 'How do you like our home, Mrs Temple? You must allow Danny to show you round before dinner.'

'I'd love that,' said Steve. 'Was that a Matisse I glimpsed in the library?'

'Yes, and there's a Utrillo behind the door. But they aren't all old masters. I bought a Lowrie last time I was in –'

'I'll show her the lot, Julia,' interrupted Danny. 'Just let Steve get her breath back after the drive. The poor girl hasn't recovered.'

Julia chuckled and began talking about the weather. Geneva was a shade dull in the winter, she admitted apologetically, not at all the same as St Moritz, and to make matters worse the authorities turned off that fountain at the end of summer. But it was better than living in Little Rock, after all.

'I was born in Alabama,' she drawled theatrically. 'Hence the accent.'

When Steve had been taken off to view the house Julia Carrington poured more drinks and then walked across to the window. 'Mr Temple, I owe you an apology, and I just don't know how to begin.' She turned with a sad smile to face him. 'I sent Danny all the way to London, just to see you, and . . .' The smile disappeared. 'As it turns out, it was quite unnecessary.'

'I understood from Danny that you'd received some particularly nasty letters. That you were being threatened with blackmail.'

'I thought so at the time.' Her gaze was direct and calculating. 'But perhaps Danny tends to exaggerate a little. That's the trouble.' She turned away to stare at the haze of light through the window. 'However, there's nothing for you to worry about, Mr Temple. I'll pay your usual fee and all expenses –'

'Miss Carrington, I'm not interested in the financial aspect of this affair. But I would like to know why you were worried enough to send Danny all the way to England to fetch me.'

She hesitated, and then sat in the chair beside him. 'All right. I received several unpleasant letters. Naturally I was worried.' She paused to give him another direct stare. 'Then yesterday morning quite by accident I discovered that the letters were written by a man who used to work for me. I simply threatened him with legal action, of course, and so he came to me and apologised.'

'It was as simple as that,' Paul murmured.

'I'm afraid it was.' The stare was faintly challenging. 'I'm terribly sorry, Mr Temple. I do feel guilty about dragging you and your delightful wife across to Switzerland. I would have sent a telegram, but you were in mid-channel –'

'There's nothing for you to feel guilty about, Miss Carrington. We both love Switzerland and we were coming here anyway. I'm sure my wife will insist that we stay here for several more days, so if you change your mind about the man who used to work for you . . .'

'I always prefer to forget the past, Mr Temple. But it's sweet of you to be so understanding.' She took Paul's hand. 'Let's go through and see whether dinner is served. I told cook eight o'clock.'

'I'm going to St Moritz,' Paul continued as they entered the dining room. 'I expect Steve will insist on a few visits to the ski slopes, although I'm mainly concerned to make enquiries about a man called Carl Milbourne. I expect you've heard of him?'

Paul felt her hand momentarily tauten. 'Milbourne?'

'He was killed last month in a car accident.'

'I think I remember. I read about him somewhere. An English publisher, wasn't he?'

'That's right. He visited you just before he died.'

'I believe he did.'

She sat at the table, and as Paul adjusted her chair she glanced up at him.

'But I didn't see him. I make a rule never to see publishers. The poor man thought I was writing my memoirs. As if I'd spend my time living in the past. I couldn't bear it. I hate watching my old movies, and as for thinking about those days in New York –'

Steve returned at that moment with Danny. They had clearly enjoyed their tour, and for the next half hour, through the avocado pear and the American-style grill, Steve and Julia talked about the collection of pottery. Steve had thrown a few pots the summer after she had left art school, but had given it up and gone back to design when she realised that she was no Wedgwood, nor even a Spode.

'I'm rather attached to my Spode,' Julia said indulgently. 'Next time you come to dinner we might get it out. Unless you present me with a Steve Temple set for Christmas.'

'After all this time,' Steve said with a laugh, 'if I made a plate the bread rolls would roll off it! I'll stick to designing books and publicity. I'll design the jacket for your autobiography when you write it.'

'Julia isn't going to,' Paul intercepted.

'Oh, but I thought –'

'And I've no intention of making a come-back,' said Julia. 'I just can't convince people I really do want to be left alone, I'm always being pestered by newspapers and publishers.'

'And film people,' Paul added.

'Film people are the worst. They're absolutely un-snubbable. I wonder now how I stood all those dreary little egotists.'

'Why do you bother to give them interviews?' asked Paul.

She stared at Paul in surprise. 'But I never see them! Danny takes care of all that nonsense for me. Don't you, darling?'

'Poor old Vince,' murmured Paul. 'He thinks he's having a personal interview with you tomorrow morning.'

'Vince?' she repeated. 'I don't know anybody called Vince.'

'He's a film director. Vince Langham.'

Her eyes flashed dangerously as she turned to Danny. 'Did you tell this film director I'd see him?'

Paul cut in quickly to avoid a scene. 'Vince told me that he spoke to you, Julia, on the telephone. But you know how film people 'exaggerate. He's so enthusiastic about persuading you to star in *Too Young to Die* that he –'

'What a dreadful title!' She pushed away her plate and glared at 'Rochester'. 'I've lost my appetite. What is *Too Young to Die*? Is it a play?'

'No, it's a novel –'

'I've never heard of it. And I've never heard of this director, Vince Langtry, or whatever he calls himself!'

'Vince Langham,' Paul said softly.

But he let the subject drop. Clearly nobody had ever persuaded Julia to do anything she hadn't wished to do, and trifling matters such as the truth about Langham's appointment or the threatening letters would change from day to day as her mood changed. Julia cheered up a little during the dessert course, and when they had drunk three cups of coffee and three glasses of Cointreau she became positively mellow. She talked nostalgically of Robert Newton and of the sex life of an English director who had been in Hollywood at the time of her last film.

'That proves she likes you,' said Danny in the car afterwards. He seemed immensely pleased with the success of the evening. 'I mean, she talked to you, didn't she, and she talked about those English guys because she knew you were English. She knew you'd have heard of Robert Newton.'

'We enjoyed coming out here to dinner,' said Steve, 'even though there isn't any mystery for Paul to solve.'

'I'm not so sure about that,' Paul began. 'God, Danny, do you have to drive so fast? I'm not quite sober enough to distinguish the road from the soft shoulder.'

'That was the soft shoulder. Sorry, folks, but it wasn't my fault. A patch of ice.'

'So slow down, eh?' Paul waited until they were down to fifty miles an hour. 'Danny, tell me, did you actually see the blackmail letters? Or did Julia tell you about them?'

'She showed them to me. But I didn't read them. She wouldn't let me.' He glanced in the driving mirror and increased his speed again.

'How long have you lived in Switzerland, Danny?' asked Steve.

'About four years. Julia bought a house in the south of France originally, but then she decided to . . .' He swung the car off the motorway without warning and without slowing down. It was a filter road leading down into Geneva, and as they sped past the more conventional traffic Danny watched over his shoulder.

'Who do you imagine is following us?' Paul asked when he was sitting upright once more.

'Nobody. Just my imagination, I expect.' He had to drive more slowly in the city traffic. 'Yeah, I was telling you about our life in the South of France.'

'I wouldn't bother,' said Paul. 'Why not just concentrate on breaking the Swiss speed records? Or alternatively you could tell me who was chasing us.'

'I've already admitted that was my imagination.'

Paul sighed. 'All right. And the suitcase that fell on your head, was that imagination? Did you imagine you saw somebody who scared the hell out of you on board the channel ferry?' They drew up outside the hotel. Paul got out of the car and leaned down by the driver's window. 'I'm sorry, Danny but I think you've been intimidated.'

'I'm easily intimidated,' said Danny with a grin. 'When Julia tells me that an ex-employee of hers has apologised for writing nasty letters, who am I to argue with her? She has a forgiving nature.'

Paul and Steve stood on the pavement and watched Danny drive away. They saw a Citroen come out of the side turning opposite and accelerate after him. A few moments later they heard shots in the distance.

'Was that,' Paul asked bitterly, 'my imagination, or was that gunfire?'

Chapter Eight

They watched the ambulance drive away and then turned to Walter Neider. 'Don't you think he should have gone to hospital?' asked Paul. The wreckage of the car was being towed away by a breakdown lorry. Paul was slightly unnerved by the efficient way a city could erase all traces of attempted murder.

'If Mr Clayton insists on returning home —' Neider shrugged massively.

'But he was scarcely conscious!' Paul protested.

'He insisted on returning home.'

Danny had been grazed on the temple by the bullet and his car had plunged into the side of a bridge. The blood had looked dramatic and Danny had been slumped across the front seats as if he were dead. But then as the small crowd of night people gathered to help and the police were sent for, Danny had begun to groan. He had survived.

'What I'd like to be sure of,' Paul said thoughtfully, 'is which side Danny is on.'

'How many sides are there?' asked Steve.

'I don't know.'

Neider walked with them back to the hotel. 'I know something of Mr Clayton's movements this afternoon,' he volunteered. 'He visited the hospital and saw a woman called Freda Sands. But I don't know what they discussed.'

'Come upstairs and have a drink,' said Paul. 'You can tell me about Freda Sands over a large brandy.'

Neider accepted the brandy, but his knowledge of Freda Sands was limited. He thought she was a celebrity in England, she was obviously rich, and she had been staying in Switzerland since the middle of January.

'At which hotel?' Paul asked quickly.

'The Piedmont.'

'And where had Carl Milbourne been staying when he was killed?'

Neider smiled thoughtfully. 'He stayed at the Piedmont. Is that significant?'

'It could very well be.'

Paul and Steve slept until half past ten, when they were woken by the shrill ring of the telephone. Paul reached out and answered it without opening his eyes. 'Ng?' he grunted. It passed through his mind that he hadn't had a proper eight hours since Tuesday.

'This is Julia Carrington,' said the voice at the other end of the line. 'I'm sorry, did I wake you?'

'Yes,' said Paul. 'But I suppose half past ten is a rather decadent time to be in bed. How's Danny?'

'I think he'll live. He ate a huge breakfast this morning, which indicates something. And he's terribly grateful that you were on the scene so quickly when that awful incident took place. Goodness knows who would have done such a thing. We seem to be living on the edge of a nightmare.'

'You are,' Paul said with a glance down at Steve. She burrowed beneath the bedclothes. 'I'll expect Danny to tell me a few facts and reasons when I see him next. In the meantime, Julia, you should keep him indoors during the long afternoons.'

'I will,' she murmured. 'I don't know what I'd do if he went out and got himself killed.'

As Paul hung up there was a tap on the door. Room service in the person of a pert brunette appeared with coffee and *croissants*. 'Breakfast, darling,' Paul called sadistically.

Steve poked her head out from the sheets and glared at the *croissants*. 'I'm not hungry.' She turned over and went back to sleep.

Paul looked at his watch and wondered what Vince Langham was doing. Had he gone out to interview Julia? The trouble with actresses was that you're never sure when they're acting. Paul wasn't certain whether Julia was being blackmailed, or whether she ever had been. And blackmail indicated a lurid past. He hoped that Walter Neider wouldn't discover anything too unpleasant about the woman.

The telephone rang again, and it was Margaret Milbourne sounding as agitated as ever. 'I have to see you, Mr Temple,' she announced without any polite preliminaries. 'It's vitally important!'

Paul sighed. 'I'm in Geneva.'

'So am I. I arrived this morning. Mr Temple, there's something I must tell you!'

'Do you want to come round here to the hotel?'

'No no, I can't do that,' she said quickly. 'I'm speaking from a restaurant called Chez Maurice. Could you be here in fifteen minutes?'

'No,' said Paul. 'I'll see you there at midday.'

The Chez Maurice was a fashionable restaurant opposite the Quai des Bergues, although at this time of the year it was crowded with Swiss businessmen and a sprinkling of international diplomats. It was the quiet season, except for bankers. Paul and Steve pushed through its medieval doors as the municipal clock was striking twelve. The atmosphere inside was cosy with panelling and the bustle of waiters.

'Gosh,' said Steve, breathing deeply, 'I hadn't realised how hungry I am.'

'Let's sit as near to that blazing fire as we can get,' said Paul. 'What about Margaret Milbourne?'

'Well, I expect she'll be late. You know what women are like when they need to see someone urgently.'

'I know what women are like,' said Steve. With a delicate feminine flick she kicked Paul in the ankle.

He had done Margaret Milbourne an injustice. As he limped across to the table she appeared from the ladies' cloakroom.

'Mr Temple, I'm so glad you could come. Hello, Mrs Temple. It's really most awfully kind of you. Yes, I suppose it is lunchtime. I hadn't thought. . .'

She sat distractedly at the table looking younger and more attractive than she had when Paul last saw her. The sable furs and the boots made her look smaller. As she spoke Paul couldn't help contrasting her with Julia Carrington. The RADA voice and the English understatement, the minimal gestures, indicated a small reserve of strength and privacy.

'How on earth did you know where we were staying?' Steve had asked. 'I don't remember Paul telling you –'

'I knew you were in Geneva, Mrs Temple, so I decided to ring all the main hotels.' She turned tensely to Paul. 'Mr Temple, I told you my husband was alive, didn't I?'

'You said you thought he was alive.'

'Well, I was right,' she said defiantly. 'He is. I've spoken to him!'

'Are you certain?' Paul asked in astonishment.

'Absolutely. He telephoned me last night. The phone rang just before dinner and the operator said there was a personal call from Geneva for me.' Her manner was of a woman vindicated against earth-bound sceptics. 'It was Carl. He sounded tense and worried, but I couldn't mistake my husband's voice.'

'Of course not,' Steve affirmed. She turned to Paul: 'No woman could, darling.'

Paul nodded reluctantly. 'What did your husband say?'

'He told me to catch a plane and meet him here, at this restaurant at eleven o'clock.'

Paul looked at the clock above the fireplace. 'It's now a quarter past twelve, Mrs Milbourne.'

'Yes, I know,' she said sadly.

They ordered their meal and Mrs Milbourne filled in the time with small talk about the fog in London and the last time she had visited Geneva with Carl. But always she came back to the miracle of the telephone call.

'Have you told your brother about the call?'

'No,' she said. 'I couldn't. He left London by train before the fog lifted. He was off to St Moritz.'

'I thought you might have seen him in Geneva.'

She looked surprised. 'But Maurice is nowhere near Geneva.'

Paul realised that Lonsdale had been as secretive with his sister as he had been with everyone else 'We met Maurice on the train out here. He said he had some business in Geneva before he moved on to St Moritz.'

'I didn't realise that,' she said thoughtfully. 'He told me . . .' She continued eating in silence.

The regular customers came and went. Paul watched them while Steve concentrated on her food and Margaret Milbourne waited for her husband.

'Carl's not coming, is he?' she said at last. 'It's obvious he isn't coming or he would have been here –'

'Excuse me, madam,' said the head waiter. 'Are you Mrs Milbourne?' He was carrying a telephone in his hand.

'Yes?' she said tensely.

'You're wanted on the telephone, madam.' He bent down and plugged the cable into a socket by the table.

'Who is it calling?' Paul asked quickly.

'The gentleman didn't give his name, sir. He is calling from St Moritz.' The head waiter picked up the receiver and murmured, 'A call for Mrs Milbourne on this extension, please.' Then he handed the phone to Margaret.

'Carl, where are you?' she asked immediately. 'I've been waiting for you!'

The voice at the other end was explaining that he'd had to go out to St Moritz. Paul leaned forward and tried to hear.

'Carl, what's this all about? You must tell me!'

'I'm sorry, dear. I was hoping we could meet, that's why I sent for you. I really did want to see you, Margaret, believe me –'

'I'll come out to St Moritz,' she said desperately. 'I'll do anything you want, Carl!'

'There's been a hitch,' said the voice. 'You'll have to go back to London. I'll be in touch as soon as I can.'

'But Carl, you can't leave me stranded in Switzerland like this! You must tell me –' Her voice rose hysterically. 'Carl! Carl, are you there?' But there was only the dialling tone.

'He's gone,' murmured Paul.

She replaced the receiver. 'Did you hear that?' she asked in a whisper. 'He wants me to go back to London.' Her shoulders quivered as she struggled with her tears, and then she was crying. 'He said there had been a hitch.'

*

Walter Neider listened unhappily. 'When Sir Graham Forbes told me you were coming, Temple, I knew there would be trouble. Forbes doesn't know anybody who lives a simple and uncomplicated life!' He turned for solace to stare at the lake. 'I had a small sandwich and a fruit juice for lunch, while you were dining luxuriously at the Chez Maurice! And what happens? You establish that Carl Milbourne is still alive! You should have sent down for a sandwich.'

'Did you trace the call?' asked Paul Temple.

'The operator in St Moritz had it recorded. But it was made from a public call box.'

Paul shrugged. 'I thought as much.'

'I have been through the documents relating to the accident,' said Neider, 'and I do not believe what you say makes sense. Nothing links the driver of the car to anybody you have mentioned. The driver is a Zurich banker of the highest respectability. He knows nothing of publishing and has read nothing but balance sheets in years.'

'Possibly not,' said Paul.

'And another thing, Temple. Where is the motive for this? Why should Carl Milbourne pretend to be dead? Who was the beneficiary under his will?'

'Margaret Milbourne,' said Paul. 'He would have made a will, but Margaret Milbourne objected.'

Neider raised a bushy eyebrow. 'Is she going to St Moritz with you this evening?'

'She keeps changing her mind,' said Paul. 'But I think she'll come with us in the end. We'll all be in St Moritz at around quarter past one tomorrow.'

'Thirteen seventeen to be exact.' Neider smiled at the effect of his precision. 'Don't be surprised if you bump into two friends of yours. Julia Carrington has a villa near there, a very beautiful villa not far from Pontresina.'

'Have you seen Julia?'

'I drove out to see her first thing this morning. She was making a great fuss of her secretary. She seems to think he'll be safer in St Moritz, although she wouldn't say what from.'

Chapter Nine

It was a spectacular journey by rail to St Moritz. The tunnels ran straight into the sides of mountains, through the rocks and out across broad plains of snow, across suicidal bridges, and far below them in the distance Swiss villages were clearly, neatly defined. Paul watched the scenery and thought about the ice age. He wondered whether the sun had been so crystalline in those days.

'I'd like to retire to Switzerland,' said Margaret Milbourne. 'I suppose that's one of the drawbacks of being a retired English actress instead of a Hollywood queen. I have to make do with Richmond.'

'Won't you be running your husband's publishing firm?' asked Paul.

'No, because Carl is still –'

'Mrs Milbourne, if Carl is still alive then he obviously doesn't wish the fact to be known. He's made perfectly certain that he remains legally dead. I wonder what his reasons are.' He continued quickly as she tried to protest. 'No no, listen. Why do you think he wants the world to think that he's dead? Was he in some kind of trouble?'

'I don't know.' She watched the countryside and her expression was of something like despair. 'Perhaps I don't care any more.'

Paul wondered briefly what she meant by that. It was obviously a private conversation she was holding with herself. 'Wouldn't he expect you to look after the firm?' he insisted.

Her interest in the passing view faltered. 'I couldn't,' she said unhappily. 'Have you met Ben Sainsbury and Norman Wallace? The well-known pantomime horse. They terrify me. I'll do the same as Carl did, and let them run the firm. After all, they know the publishing jungle.'

'I thought they were rather a jolly pair,' Steve said rashly, 'a double act like Laurel and Hardy.'

'Jolly? They're much more like Burke and Hare. Norman Wallace is all charm and efficiency, and he alternates with Ben's bluster and rage, so together they always get their way. You can never win an argument with Ben Sainsbury because next morning when he's sober he forgets that any argument took place. I used to want Carl to give him the sack, but Carl didn't dare. He was scared that Ben would go.'

'That's a thought,' said Steve, 'they could set up on their own; Wallace and Sainsbury, the old firm.'

'Good lord no,' said Paul. 'Ben wouldn't set up his own firm. That would make him a capitalist!'

Margaret Milbourne laughed for the first time in four weeks.

The train pulled into the station and they went off to the Grison House Hotel. 'It strikes me,' Steve said as she began unpacking, 'that we're not having much of a holiday. I think I'm going to rebel.' She left the clothes strewn on the bed and went across to the window.

'What form will the rebellion take?' Paul asked.

'I'm going skiing!'

'But I have to visit the hat shop –'

'Look at those slopes! See all those dots creeping down into the valley? Whoever visited St Moritz and didn't go skiing!?'

Paul shrugged. 'Whatever you say, darling. Why don't you take Margaret Milbourne with you? I'd rather she wasn't tagging along with me to the shop. I expect she'd look very glamorous in a hat with a bobble on it.'

'She doesn't look the skiing type to me,' Steve said with a laugh.

'Then she can watch.'

Steve shook her head. 'I'll take her off somewhere for a couple of hours, but then you're coming down those slopes with me. Dammit, what do you think I married you for?'

'Because of my grand slalom?' asked Paul.

The hat shop, as it turned out, was a small Swiss equivalent of Fortnum and Mason that sold everything from hats to elephants. Paul amused himself as he went up to the third floor by wondering whether this was where Hannibal had bought his troupe, or whether those particular elephants had been breeding ever since.

'God dammit!' someone shouted.

There was a clatter across the store while Paul was passing through the sports section and a pile of skates fell on to a man whose feet were flailing in skis. His head was buried beneath the boxes, but there was no mistaking the scruffy trousers and the American accent muttering 'Hell's bells!' It was Vince Langham.

'I'm the only man who can break a leg *buying* a pair of skis,' he said when Paul had dug him out. 'I never even mastered the roller skates I had for my eighth birthday.'

'What are you doing in St Moritz?' Paul asked while he brushed some of the dust from his baggy jacket. 'Are you following me?'

'If I'm following you I'm the most conspicuous tail in the business,' he laughed. 'I thought you were following me.'

'Never.'

Vince stared at him disbelievingly. 'Oh well. I'm here because Julia Carrington is in St Moritz. And where Julia goes there go I. Just to save you too much sleuthing.'

'I thought you had an appointment –'

'So did I.' Vince left the skis in the centre of the floor where he had fallen. 'That slimy little Machiavelli must have set to work on her as soon as he got back. I'd like to murder Danny Clayton.'

Paul shook his head. 'Why not admit the truth, Vince? Julia had never heard of you when I mentioned your phone call. She didn't even know your name.'

Vince pushed his unkempt hair back over his collar. 'Paul, I despair of you. Would I tell a lie? One of the best films Julia made was called *The Shadow of Fear*. It was a brilliant dramatic performance. Do you remember the film?'

'Of course,' said Paul. 'I was young and impressionable –'

'I directed the Goddammed thing!'

'It wasn't as good as the films you've made in Europe.'

'What are you trying to do, prove me a liar?' he asked wearily. 'Would that make me a killer or something? Listen, I'm a simple film-maker, I bought a book and now I'm trying to find my leading actress. It's a hard enough business setting up a film without people solving mysteries all around me.'

'All right,' Paul said apologetically.

'Who'd be a film director? Do you know, last year I was making a film in the middle east and the Arab-Israeli war broke out again! It's enough to make a man give up!'

He went off muttering in search of the novice ski run. The man was a liar; but perhaps it was all in the cause of filmmaking. Paul continued his search for the manager's office. It was at the rear of the building.

'Mr Paul Temple, the author?' asked the manager politely. 'I'm delighted to meet you, Mr Temple. I never read books myself, but you do very well in our book department. Let me take you down to meet the manager –'

'Thank you,' said Paul. 'But I really came because –'

'A Mr Neufeld, most enthusiastic. He sometimes manages to persuade eminent authors to make a personal appearance, sign copies of their books. Will you be staying long in St Moritz?'

'No,' Paul said quickly. 'Mr Kroner, I'm making some enquiries about a man who was killed in this town last month. I hope you might be able to help me.'

Kroner gave an ironic smile. 'I have a very bad memory.'

There was a pause. 'Some of the most famous novelists have sat in what Herr Neufeld calls his hot seat.'

Paul laughed and agreed to sign copies of his books.

'Mr Neufeld will be honoured, Mr Temple. So how can I help you?'

'A month ago a man named Carl Milbourne bought a hat from this store and asked for his old hat to be posted back to an address in London.'

Kroner nodded. 'I would have no personal knowledge of the transaction. But there's probably a record of it in the hat department.'

'Do you think I could have a word with the assistant?' Paul asked.

Kroner browsed through a card index. 'Unfortunately that won't be possible, Mr Temple. At that time the assistant in the hat department was an Italian girl who has since returned to Naples. We take on a great number of extra staff just before

Christmas, you will understand.' He thought for a moment, and then smiled. 'But wait a moment. Perhaps I do recall the transaction. The assistant came and asked me if it was possible to post your friend's hat to England, I believe. The idea was new to her. She fetched me out to have a word with the customer.'

Paul took the photograph of Carl Milbourne from his wallet. 'Would this be the man, Mr Kroner?'

Kroner stared at the photograph. 'It is very difficult, we have so many tourists –'

'Here are some more photographs,' said Paul, spreading them on the desk. 'Do you recognise –?'

'I couldn't be really certain. However, there was something else, Mr Temple. I don't know whether it is useful, but as I remember, your friend was not alone. He was with a party of people.' He smiled at the feat of memory. 'Is that not so?'

'Well, it's possible, I suppose, although –'

'A group of tourists, Mr Temple. They were all laughing and joking together, making quite a noise.'

'With Mr Milbourne? Did you see anyone actually speak to him?'

'Ah,' said Kroner, 'that I can't remember. But I certainly formed the impression he was with them.'

Paul went towards the door feeling rather pleased with himself. 'You've been most helpful, Mr Kroner.' The cheerful little man was striding along beside him. As they passed back through the sports department Paul said, 'I must give you a ring about the autograph session . . .' Mr Kroner joined him in the lift.

On the ground floor he saw Steve and Mrs Milbourne laden with parcels making for the restaurant. Paul noted the new sunglasses, new hat with inappropriate ear flaps and fur boots. Maybe he should sign a lot of books, Paul reflected, before asking what the parcels contained.

'Herr Neufeld's department is through here . . .'

Maurice Lonsdale was waiting for them at a table by the window. He was still, thought Steve, the essence of an English financier, right down to the buttonhole. They sat beside him.

'Steve is off skiing this afternoon,' said Margaret. 'Of course the slopes of St Moritz are gentle enough, but it makes one nostalgic.'

'Have you done much skiing?' asked Lonsdale in surprise.

'Before I married Carl,' she said. 'Darling, don't you remember? I used to enjoy the run from Gornergrat to Zermatt. I suppose that was ten years ago now.'

'I never could keep up with your activities, Margaret,' he said with a sigh. 'I thought your idea of a holiday was lying in the sun.'

'Always the cynic,' Margaret sighed. She picked up her bag and went off in search of the ladies' room. 'Don't eat the whole of that sausage while I'm gone.'

Steve smiled. 'Any news of your friend Miss Sands?' she asked politely.

'Freda?' He looked startled at her good memory. 'Yes, I'm afraid the news isn't good. I thought it was just a broken leg, but apparently the poor darling slipped a disc as well. She's in a great deal of pain.'

'I suppose you cheered her up?'

'Oh well, a bunch of grapes, you know, and a few magazines.' He leaned confidentially across the table. 'Margaret's feeling the strain, you know, she really is. If I'd been at home I'd have done my damnedest to have prevented her from coming out here.'

'You don't believe Carl is alive?'

Lonsdale gave one of his superior smiles. 'Well, if he is alive, then who was the dead man? Why was he wearing Carl's clothes and carrying his papers?'

'That, as the politicians say, is a good question.'

'They only say that when they know the answers.' His manner suddenly dropped the assumption of male superiority and he seemed genuinely worried. 'Do you know the answers, Mrs Temple?'

'I'm afraid I don't.' She smiled as well just in case her dislike of the man was showing. 'But then, I'm no politician.'

'Carl was in Geneva on a perfectly straightforward business trip, to see Julia Carrington. For the life of me I fail to see why he should have become involved in all this mystery.' He glanced over his shoulder to see whether Margaret was coming. 'Mrs Temple, tell me, what does your husband make of it? He must have some idea by now of what's behind it all.'

'I'm afraid that like most husbands Paul doesn't always confide in me,' said Steve.

'I don't believe that.' He pointed his fork at her. 'I'm sorry to disillusion you, Mrs Temple, but I'm afraid you are a politician.' Luckily Margaret returned before he could start waving the *schlueblig* about.

'Darling, do you know who I've just seen? Paul was in the books department helping them put up a poster.'

'He's very good with a pot of paste,' said Steve. 'What did the poster say?'

'It was in German. Something about *der Autor* signing his *Bucher* next week. I must say he looked rather abashed.' She sighed. 'I used to enjoy personal appearances. I once spent a fortnight going round local cinemas, making a little speech and thanking God for the British film industry. It kept one in touch with the British public.' She ate briefly and then turned to her brother. 'By the way, darling, Paul said he wants to talk with you.'

'Is he going to join us?'

'Yes, but he wants to talk with you privately. I suppose he means away from me. You really have convinced everybody that I'm an hysterical woman. But you know now – I was right, wasn't I?'

'Tell me, Temple, was it really Carl on the telephone?'

'Your sister certainly seemed to think so.'

Paul looked in the bar mirror at Steve and Mrs Milbourne talking animatedly at their table. The sound of her husband's voice had made her more sure of herself and in some ways more worried. She was a woman in trouble who didn't quite know what the trouble was.

'It's unbelievable,' said Lonsdale.

'Yes. How do you find the brandy?' It was the best. 'Lonsdale, there's something I've been meaning to ask you. Had your brother-in-law any worries? Financial worries?'

'No more than most businessmen,' he said with a laugh. 'I gather publishing has its recesses and its booms. At one time Milbourne & Co. were having a tough time, but that passed.'

'So you don't think he'd be likely to – well, to fake the accident and then disappear? Such things have happened. Men who have been officially dead have been known to live for years on their insurance money.'

Lonsdale laughed easily. 'Carl was the most under-insured man I know. There was a policy, but Margaret has refused to claim on it. She still believes . . .' He put more soda into the brandy, which made Paul wince. 'No, it hasn't happened in this case. If Carl had been desperate he'd have come to me, or one of his friends.'

'Did he ever come to you? Did he ever borrow money from you?'

'Yes, as a matter of fact he did.' Lonsdale talked casually, as if it were a normal business matter. 'I sank forty thousand pounds in his firm about six months ago. But it's safe enough. I'm not worried. Will you have another drink?'

'No thanks, I'm skiing this afternoon. I'll need a clear head if I'm to survive.'

Chapter Ten

Paul and Steve travelled to the top of the first slopes by bus and then went on by funicular. Steve looked glamorous in her new sheepskin coat. She sat in the corner of the suspended carriage like an expensive model on her way to be photographed in the snow. Paul wondered how she managed to make ski pants, parka and boots look so elegant.

'Perhaps I should have bought one of those woollen hats,' Paul suggested, 'with a bobble. Then people would know I belong with you.'

'You spent a much more useful morning, darling,' said Steve, with a critical glance at his peaked cap. 'You established that Carl Milbourne had joined up with a party of tourists.'

'I didn't.' He paused thoughtfully. 'I think it's possible that the man who bought the hat was trying to avoid attention by tacking himself on to a group of tourists.'

'And why should he want to avoid attention?' Steve asked brightly. 'Because he wasn't Carl Milbourne? But Margaret was positive –'

'Margaret Milbourne is a very good actress. She always was.'

'Are you suggesting that she –?' Steve began in disbelief. 'No no, I like Margaret Milbourne. I enjoyed my morning

113

with her, in spite of the way she projects her personality all the time. I felt sorry for her when Maurice Lonsdale told her she had to go back to London.'

'Did they quarrel?' asked Paul.

'Not really. Lonsdale just told her to keep out of the way. She was rather upset, but of course her husband had already told her to do just that. If it was her husband.'

The funicular came to a stop. Paul looked back down the cable stretching into the valley and wondered why they bothered to come all this way just to ski back in five and a half minutes. There was a blizzard blowing up and he began to wish he had taken his clothing as seriously as Steve had.

'Ah well,' he murmured languidly, 'we'll whizz down once and straight back to the hotel for a hot bath.'

'You don't get off as lightly as that,' she said with a toss of her head. 'When we've been down Piz Nair we'll have a go from Trais Fluors.'

'We shan't have time,' said Paul. 'We're dining with Julia Carrington tonight, which is quite a journey –'

'All right, but we don't go back till it's dark.'

Steve set off along the peak before he could argue, away from the party of Americans who had travelled up with them. A stray middle-aged man in rimless dark glasses tagged along behind them and the funicular began to shudder its way back down. They spent several minutes getting into their skis, testing their bindings and exchanging friendly smiles with the stray fat man.

'Good afternoon, Paul Temple,' he said loudly and slowly. 'Famous man, ha ha! My name Ferdy. No famous man, ha ha ha!'

Paul was surprised. 'Good afternoon, Ferdy.'

114

'This is the BBC foreign service broadcasting from London, and here is the news.' The man roared with laughter. 'Good English, yes?'

'Very good,' said Paul. 'Radio One is Wonderful.'

The man transpired to be an Italian from Verona. He had no grammar but an excellent memory and they established a relationship with the phrases he had learnt from listening to the radio. 'An official spokesman said today,' he declaimed solemnly, 'a depression is moving in from Faroe and Shannon.'

Their skis firm, goggles in place, ski-sticks clutched nervously, they began to sidestep along the packed snow of the ridge. The blizzard was increasing lower down the slopes, but Paul seemed to remember that experts consider a blizzard good for skiing. St Moritz looked an awfully long way off.

'Coming?' called Steve, and she was away.

The Italian held out his gloved hand to Paul. 'Thank you for practising my English.' They shook hands. 'Manchester United three nil.' He pushed at his ski sticks and slithered off in pursuit of Steve. His roar of laughter was dispersed in the wind.

Paul rapidly picked up speed and within a hundred yards he was feeling the old exhilaration; he had always enjoyed the gale rushing at him, the sensation of flying across the mountains. He tried out a few simple manoeuvres, leaning forward, using the snowplough to slow down, developing his body rhythm and then traversing the line of fall. It was easy, and he was gaining on Steve.

Gratifying to find one was still good at it, he thought. Perhaps skiing was like riding a bicycle – once learned, never quite forgotten. A few tentative sideslips and he felt like a champion.

There was no hope of catching up with Ferdy, but the Italians have alps of their own. Ferdy probably spent all his free time skiing, when he wasn't listening to the English radio. Paul drew level with Steve a few moments later.

'You're doing quite well,' he called patronisingly, although she probably didn't hear him. Her eyes were fixed intently on the virgin snow twenty yards ahead.

They were coming into the blizzard when Paul noticed two sudden spurts of snow erupt beside their skis. 'Don't look now, darling,' he called fancifully, 'but we're being fired at.'

Steve looked over her shoulder and they smiled at each other. The crack of a pistol shot reverberated across the valley. Their smiles faltered. Ferdy was passing the clump of trees down to their right and he crumpled to the ground.

Steve had raised her ski-stick to point at a figure lurking in the trees, which didn't seem the most sensible way to cope with the situation. She veered towards the danger, increased speed and crouched on her skis. The marksman took another shot and then disappeared from sight.

'You look after Ferdy!' Paul shouted.

Paul circuited the trees and swooped down to the point where the man with the gun should have been. But he was two hundred yards below, moving rapidly across the slope to the knot of Americans who were skidding clumsily about in the distance. There was no hope of catching him.

And the gear didn't help identification. Goggles and fur hat, bulky sweater. It could have been anybody, anybody of normal build and height, even a woman. Paul cursed himself for being out of practice and cruised back to find Steve attending the wounded Ferdy.

'He'll be all right,' said Steve. 'The bullet grazed his leg and scared him half to death.'

'Blood,' said Ferdy pointing in horror at the stain on the snow. 'Who would do such a thing, Paul Temple?'

'I'm sorry,' said Paul. 'Just one of the dangers of being on a ski slope with me.'

'Did you see who it was?' asked Steve.

'No,' Paul said when he had his breath back. 'The trees are pretty thick over there, and our friend disappeared into the blizzard with twenty-four Americans.'

Paul went across to the clump of trees where they had first seen the gunman. Something yellow was reflecting the light. Among the anonymous ski tracks there was a gold cigarette case. It was lying on the surface of the snow, obviously dropped in the last few minutes.

There were no cigarettes inside, but an inscription in the lid read, *To V with love from J.* So it belonged to V. Paul wrapped it carefully in his handkerchief, although he doubted whether they would have time to check on fingerprints.

'Well, well,' said Steve. 'Now who do we know –?'

Paul shook his head. 'I know what you're thinking, darling. But I can't see Vince Langham shooting at anyone, unless it's from behind a camera. Come on, let's get Ferdy back on his runners.'

'Do you think it was dropped accidentally?' she asked. 'Or was it planted?'

'That's a good question.'

They lifted Ferdy to his feet and adjusted his hat. He was still very nervous. It seemed to Ferdy a fine distinction, when people were messing about with guns, between a graze on the leg and a bullet in the heart. 'I am not accustomed to cowboys and Indians,' he said severely.

117

Chapter Eleven

Paul had a shower before venturing out into the winter again. He would have preferred a normal bath because he had some thinking to do. But the stream of almost boiling water was toning up the muscles and convinced him that perhaps it was better to be fit than philosophical. He would let Steve do the thinking.

'Do you want me to scrub your back?' she asked.

'You'll get drenched.'

She sat by the shower curtain and stared up at Paul as he contorted to scrub his own back. 'I had an awful thought,' she confessed, 'when fat little Ferdy was shot: I was glad, because the gunman was obviously meaning to shoot you.'

Paul nodded. 'If there were any justice in this world I'd have been killed years ago.'

'Poor little Ferdy.'

'Well, I thought he made rather a fuss,' said Paul.

'Bully for him!' Steve said vigorously. 'I wish you were more like that. What on earth is this case all about, and why should you risk your life for it? It doesn't make sense.' She stood up and fetched the towel. 'Why don't you come out of that shower and come to bed? I think I'm still in love with you.'

'We're having dinner with Julia Carrington in half an hour.'

'Is that important?' She laughed provocatively. 'I think I'll come in the shower with you –'

'Steve, you're fully dressed!' He quickly turned off the taps. 'Steve, behave yourself. The hotel staff will think we aren't married.'

She pouted and went across to sit on the bed. She had kept hold of the towel. 'Why do we have to have dinner with Julia?'

'I don't know why she wants to see me again,' said Paul coming out of the shower, 'but I know why I need to see her.' He stood with his arms out for Steve to wrap the towel round his waist.

'How does she fit into this Milbourne business?'

'She's at the absolute centre of it.'

'I see.' Steve contemplated the lithe body as he dried himself. 'Do you think that Carl Milbourne was blackmailing her? That would fit, wouldn't it, with the letters she received and the odd circumstances of his visit. Maybe Danny Clayton killed him.' She looked unhappy. 'That would be neat, but it doesn't fit with my understanding of Danny. Does it fit with Carl Milbourne?'

'No,' said Paul, 'not if he's still alive.'

'He's had money troubles with his firm.'

Paul smiled encouragingly. 'And why did Julia pretend not to know of Vince Langham?'

'Yes, that's a mystery, isn't it? I've been wondering about those two.' She took a rather lurid tie from the clothes laid out on the bed and replaced it with a sober blue one. 'Darling, do you think she would have been the J who gave Vince that gold cigarette case?'

'An expensive present.'

'Oh, I don't know. It's expensive, but a star like Julia might well have given something like that to her director at the end of a film.'

The telephone rang by the bed. It was the reception desk to announce that Paul's car had arrived to take them to the Villa Serbolini. Paul said they would be down in five minutes and continued dressing.

'Don't you think it might have been Vince Langham out there on the ice cap?' asked Steve.

'No. If it were,' he said with a laugh, 'Vince must have had some damned good coaching since this morning. Just trying on a pair of skis he nearly wrecked the shop. But I think you're right about one thing, darling, the J was for Julia.'

He took her arm, gave her a kiss, and led her from the hotel. It was nice to have somebody so attractive to do one's thinking. It was a shame they had to go out in the snow.

It took them more than half an hour to drive to Pontresina. The blizzard was raging now and the roads were becoming impassable snowdrifts. Steve huddled in the corner of the limousine swathed in fur and tried to guess Danny Clayton's reason for living out here with Julia.

'Perhaps he needs a mother figure?' she wondered. But that was hardly convincing. 'Or maybe it's the money?' No, it couldn't be the money or the style of life such money could buy. People such as Danny fight their way up to achieve power. But power was exactly what he didn't have out here in Switzerland. He was more like a prisoner.

Steve looked at the high wall round the Julia Carrington estate. The house lay back in extensive grounds, like a prison. It was a lavish home, but for somebody like Danny rather suffocating. There had to be something about Danny that she didn't know.

The car had turned into the approach to the wrought iron gates with wheels spinning in the snow. The chauffeur stopped and went to open the gates.

'I think we might have to walk from here, darling,' said Paul.

The chauffeur was apologetic. 'You can see the lights through the trees, sir. It will take you two or three minutes, unless you care to wait while I clear the snow.'

'I don't think it's as cold outside as it looks,' said Paul.

'No, it couldn't possibly be.'

Paul helped her from the car and smiled at her obvious reluctance to get snow on the mauve suede boots. The essence of fashion, he reflected, was that it should be impracticable. But there was no alternative to walking. The huge gates were immovable and the drive was under swirling, thick snow. They went along to a wicket gate in the wall.

'What time shall I pick you up, sir?' asked the chauffeur.

'Oh, about ten thirty,' he said. The wicket gate opened easily into the grounds. 'Come on, Steve, you can change your clothes when we get to the house.'

'Huh! I'll look like Blanche Dubois in Julia's clothes.'

In fact Paul was enjoying the walk. The snow settled on their faces, freezing to their eyebrows and anaesthetising their jaws so that they had to proceed in silence. Paul flashed his pencil torch occasionally at the stone peacocks, urns and heads that lined the drive, but he could only see them as yellow blurs. The crunch of packed snow beneath their feet was the only sound until they heard a scream over to their right.

'I could have sworn I heard someone shouting –' Steve began.

The scream was repeated.

'Stay here, darling,' said Paul. 'If I need any help you'll be able to –'

'Not on your life!' She plunged into the undergrowth behind Paul. 'I'm coming with you!'

The low moaning sound was consistent enough to guide them towards the injured man. Paul flashed his torch at the bushes as they hurried past until eventually they reached a clearing. A set of footprints was clearly visible, made by somebody running towards the house.

Paul looked uncertainly in that direction, undecided about giving chase or helping the injured. The moaning was becoming more faint, so Paul followed the direction from which the footprints had been running. He paused where the man running had clearly paused and looked about. Perhaps this was where he had been when he had heard Paul and Steve crashing towards him. Perhaps he had thrown away the dark object lying over there in the snow.

'Darling,' Steve called, 'over here! I think I've found him!'

Paul bent down by a clump of ornamental shrubbery and with his gloved hands he picked up a common sheath knife. The sort of thing boy scouts carry, except that this one was covered in blood. Paul wrapped it in another handkerchief and then hurried over to Steve.

'Who is he?' he asked.

'I'm not sure.'

The man had been writhing in the snow and was now half buried beneath a snowdrift. There was blood everywhere, from the gash in his thick flying jacket. Paul scooped the body clear and turned him over, brushing the snow from his face and slightly lifting his head.

'Vince,' he murmured, 'can you hear me?'

'God, it hurts, Paul,' he gasped in obvious agony. 'It's my back. A knife. . .'

Paul gave the torch to Steve and indicated the house. She ran off across the snow to fetch help.

'Don't worry, Vince, we'll soon have you in a warm bed. Try to be still.'

Paul tore a strip from his shirt and made a wad to stem the bleeding from below Vince's ribs. Then he covered the man's shivering body with his coat. His breathing was regular but painfully laboured. Paul thought he had passed out, but after they had been waiting a few minutes Vince spoke again.

'I've been meaning to tell you about Carl Milbourne –'

'It can wait.'

Paul hadn't realised how noisy a snowstorm could be. The continual swish of snow falling from branches, the low whistle of the breeze, the crackle of protesting trees heavy with ice.

'It all started with Carl Milbourne,' the voice continued weakly, 'and that bloody novel.'

'I know,' said Paul gently. I suppose you wrote *Too Young to Die*. Are you Richard Randolph?'

'How did you guess?'

'It's a bad novel,' Paul said cruelly. 'Reads like a film script.'

A slight chuckle turned to a coughing spasm. 'Well, I wrote it some time ago and sent it to Carl Milbourne. I'd dealt with him before, I bought the film rights of a book from him a few years back. And Carl liked *Too Young to Die*, he thought it was well written and he wanted to see me.' He paused to regain his strength. 'I wish I'd never seen him.'

'You shouldn't have written the novel.'

'True. I told Carl where I got the idea for the story, that was the trouble. It was while I was in Hollywood, making a picture for –' He broke off in agony.

'It's all right, don't talk,' said Paul. 'I can guess where you found the idea. It was based on something that happened to Julia Carrington.'

'Yes.' The voice in the darkness sounded surprised. 'My back hurts like hell, Paul.'

'I think somebody's coming. You won't be left here much longer.' The flicker of lanterns and the buzz of voices were approaching from the house. 'By the way, Vince, what were you doing out here this evening?'

'I had an appointment'

Paul grunted. That was a story he had heard before from Vince, and it was usually disputed. 'Are you sure?'

'Yeah, Danny Clayton phoned and said that Julia would see me. So I was on my way up to the house when someone came up behind me and –' He broke off as the group of people came across to them. 'I hope they can stop this pain, Paul, I can't bear it much longer.'

Danny stared indignantly at the sick man. 'There's some mistake, Mr Langham. I didn't phone you.'

'But you did!' He was lying in bed, deathly pale and weak, yet a flush of excitement lit his eyes. 'You told me to come here –'

The doctor raised an authoritative hand for silence. 'There must be no more talking, gentlemen. Mr Langham must have complete rest. We must leave him.'

The doctor was a daunting man who had taken over the guest room as if it were his own hospital, riding blithely over objections and discussion with imperious disdain. He had finally crushed Julia herself by saying that the whole villa would make an excellent sanatorium. He shooed them from the sickroom and turned out the lights. Paul followed the group down to the drawing-room.

Julia was looking more strained than she had been in Geneva, the slenderness was looking less regal and more like a wiry strength. 'Mr Temple,' she said irritably, 'that man was obviously lying.'

'I believe him,' Paul murmured.

'Do you mean,' she asked fiercely, 'that you don't believe Danny when he says that he didn't telephone Mr Langham?'

'I think someone telephoned Vince. If it wasn't Danny then someone must have impersonated him.'

Danny Clayton was looking nervous, as though he expected a display of artistic temperament from Julia at any moment. 'It is possible,' he said tentatively, 'although why should anyone –?'

'I find the whole business extremely annoying!' Julia flounced across to the drinks tray and refilled her glass. 'If the newspapers get hold of this story they'll assume that I invited Langham here because he's a film director . . .'

Steve sighed so audibly that the actress paused as if she had been booed. 'There's no reason,' said Steve, 'why the newspapers should get hold of the story.'

'Of course not,' Danny assured her. 'I'll have a word with Langham tomorrow. I'm sure he'll be reasonable.'

'I hope you're right.' Julia glared aggressively at Paul. 'I'm not having my life ruined by reporters.'

She was obviously in no mood to be the perfect hostess, so Paul gave her a few moments to calm down while he helped himself to a brandy. Danny hovered about as though he should be pouring the drinks but was anxious not to stray too far from Julia. The longer the silence lasted the more difficult it became for Julia to continue her scene. Eventually Paul turned to her and spoke with quiet authority.

'Would it be such a bad idea, Miss Carrington, if the newspapers were to print the whole of your story?'

'What do you mean?' she whispered.

'I think it's about time we put our cards on the table. After all, someone tried to murder Vince tonight, and they very nearly succeeded. Someone even tried to murder Danny in Geneva. I should have thought that by now you would realise how dangerous it is to pretend that nothing is happening.'

'Are you suggesting that Julia is covering up the truth?' Danny demanded loyally.

'Yes,' said Paul. 'Now don't interrupt. I'm suggesting that it's about time Miss Carrington told me about Carl Milbourne and what it was –'

'What do you know about Milbourne?' Julia asked. She had stopped acting now. She was obviously frightened.

'Carl Milbourne was blackmailing you.' Paul sat on the sofa beside her. 'Well, Julia, wasn't he blackmailing you?'

'Yes.' Her voice was almost inaudible. 'He still is.'

'I can deal with Milbourne,' said Danny with an attempt at manly self-confidence.

She shook her head.

'It started in Hollywood, didn't it?' Paul prompted. 'Many years ago when you were drinking heavily?'

She glanced pleadingly at Danny, but Danny simply held out his hands in a gesture of helplessness. She was on her own. 'Yes,' she said, 'I was drinking heavily. It's a hell of a life at the top in Hollywood. I was a symbol of success, surrounded by people who thought I was wonderful. They must have hated me, but there were too many careers and to much money invested in me. In those days Hollywood's revenge on its stars was to surround them with cheap glitter, to fill their lives with lavish parties, sex and empty excitement, meaningless power.'

Julia smiled ironically. 'I'm sorry to sound puritanical, I might have enjoyed the sex and the money if only the people had been different.'

'Believe me, Paul, it's a rat race,' Danny explained.

'I wanted to get away, but I couldn't,' Julia continued. 'It wasn't only the contracts that kept me there; I suppose in some ways I enjoyed the success – I was an actress, and some of the films I made were good films. So I was enmeshed, Mr Temple, stuck. And I'm afraid I became a little self-pitying.'

'Was that when you took to drinking?'

She nodded. 'I had a hide-out in an apartment house in Santa Barbara. I used to go there by myself at weekends. And one night, during a drinking bout, I set fire to the apartment.' She went across to refill her glass in the silence. 'I escaped, but many people lost their lives that night. Including Danny's mother and father.'

Danny took her hand encouragingly.

'I don't even remember how it happened. I suppose I was smoking and I probably fell asleep. There was an enquiry, but they didn't discover how it happened because they didn't know I was there.' She looked directly at Paul. 'I'd been to the head of the studio and told him the whole story. I wanted to accept full responsibility for what had happened. But the studio wouldn't hear of it.'

'They were halfway through a picture,' explained Danny.

'They hushed the whole thing up. The only person who knew that I was at Santa Barbara on the night of the fire was the manager of the apartment house, and the studio paid him forty thousand dollars to keep his mouth shut.' She smiled sadly. 'Not only that, they provided me with an alibi as well. The studio was capable of taking care of almost anything. They'd had plenty of practice.'

'It must have been a ghastly experience,' said Steve.

'Yes, it was. One feels so guilty, so anxious to make amends, and of course there's nothing one can do to help the people who were burned to death.'

'So,' said Danny, 'she helped the survivors.'

'I tried to take care of Danny – put him through college and get him a job at the studio. Although Danny didn't need much help from me, he was soon running the whole outfit.'

'I'm a rat,' said Danny, 'I enjoyed the rat race. Do you know, I even miss it sometimes. But Julia's pretty helpless, so when she retired a few years later I had to retire with her. It was she who needed taking care of.' He shook his head reprovingly. 'She should have let me take care of the blackmail business. I came up against worse characters than Carl Milbourne in Hollywood. I could have sorted it out!'

Paul raised an eyebrow. 'Didn't you?'

'No.'

'I was afraid to bluff it out,' said Julia. 'When Carl Milbourne came to see me six months ago he showed me the manuscript of a novel called *Too Young to Die*. As soon as I read it I knew that it was my life story, that it was based on my experiences in Hollywood.'

Paul nodded. 'Yes, Randolph heard your story from the manager of the apartment house.'

'Then he demanded money. Milbourne told me that he was Richard Randolph and that –'

'He told you he was Randolph?' Paul asked in surprise.

'Yes. Didn't you know that? Milbourne was the author and he owned all the rights in the book. Naturally I asked him not to publish it, and he agreed. Subject to certain monetary considerations.'

'How much,' asked Steve, 'did you pay Carl Milbourne?'

She thought for a moment. 'Up to the time of the accident, about forty thousand pounds.'

'I expect you were relieved,' Paul said carefully, 'when you heard about the accident.'

'Of course. I thought that would be the end of the matter. But it wasn't. A short time after it happened I had a phone call from Mrs Milbourne. She said she felt convinced that her husband was still alive, and she asked if I had heard from him.'

'What did you say?' asked Paul.

'I lied.' She shrugged her shoulders in weary resignation. 'I said I'd never even met her husband.'

'And then what happened?'

'About a week ago I had a phone call from Carl Milbourne himself. He told me I had to make one more payment of sixty thousand pounds. That was when Danny found out about the affair, and insisted on becoming involved.'

'Well, sixty thousand dollars,' Danny said indignantly.

'Did Milbourne tell you where to deliver the money?' asked Paul.

'No, he simply told me to come to St Moritz and wait. He said he would contact me here.'

'And has he?'

'No,' she sighed, 'not yet.'

'Good. That gives us time to prepare.'

'I begged Julia to go to the police,' said Danny. 'But she wouldn't hear of it. She's terrified of the law. So finally I persuaded her to see you.' He shrugged. 'Then at the very last moment, on the day you arrived –'

'She funked it,' said Paul.

'Yes.'

Julia rose to her feet. 'Well, I haven't funked it now, Mr Temple. I've told you the whole truth. Shall we go through

and have some dinner? I feel rather hungry. You can tell me
what I ought to do while we eat.'

Paul took her arm and led her through to the dining room.
'There's no doubt in my mind what you should do, Miss
Carrington,' he said firmly. 'No doubt at all.'

Steve followed behind with Danny Clayton. 'All this excitement has made me hungry as well,' she was saying. 'It's all
action in Switzerland this year, isn't it?'

Chapter Twelve

Paul had been in a strangely cryptic mood on the way back to the hotel. It had seemed to Steve that their mystery was almost solved – all they needed to know was the identity of the blackmailer and whether Carl Milbourne was really alive. But Paul was preoccupied. Perhaps it was the arctic weather.

'Darling,' she said. 'I've been wondering about Danny Clayton and that shooting incident in Geneva.'

Paul stared at the curtain of snow on the car window. 'Yes, I was wondering about that. Why should anyone want to kill Danny?'

'Well!' said Steve, 'he had been trying to persuade Julia to go to the police about being blackmailed.'

'That's what he says.'

They drove on slowly through the snow. Steve stared at the close-cropped neck of the chauffeur. She wondered whether his ears were holding up his hat. She yawned, and decided that she was tired. A shame they didn't have electric blankets in the hotel. She should have brought a hot water bottle from home.

'There is another explanation, of course,' Paul continued unexpectedly. 'Danny might have been doing a little investigating on his own behalf. We know that the first thing he did when he arrived in London was to look up Margaret Milbourne. What else did he get up to?'

'I don't know,' said Steve.

'Do you think he tried to blackmail her, as she said? Is he playing a double game?'

'I've always trusted Danny completely.' Steve thought for a moment. 'Darling, are you suggesting that Danny took over –?'

'I'm not suggesting anything, except that blackmail is contagious. I wouldn't cross Danny off our list of suspects yet, that's all.' There was another silence, and then Paul added bitterly, 'Nor would I cross off Vince Langham. We may know the story behind all this, but we're no closer to the person responsible. I'm still sceptical about them all.'

'I like Vince Langham,' Steve said regretfully.

'He was probably on the train that night Danny was beaten up,' said Paul. 'He's known Julia for years, and the chances are he knew Danny better than either of them admitted.'

Steve sighed. 'I'd much rather you pinned the whole thing on Maurice Lonsdale. He's an odious man, and what the blazes is he doing with us in St Moritz?'

He was staying at the same hotel, and the manager thought he was a friend of Paul's. As soon as the car drew up in the forecourt the manager came scurrying out to have a word with them.

'Yes,' Paul admitted, 'we know Mr Lonsdale. What on earth has he done?'

The manager was indeterminately Mediterranean, excitable and hideously discreet. 'There's been a most unfortunate accident . . .' It was clearly something too awful to mention in polite company.

Paul sent Steve ahead to their suite while he went with the manager to Lonsdale's room. Lonsdale was on the top floor at the end of the corridor; an unfashionable, inexpensive room which, as the manager explained, had been booked at very short notice.

'One of the maids went to Mr Lonsdale's room thinking it was empty,' he whispered. 'She heard groans coming from the bathroom. Poor girl, she was appalled. Mr Lonsdale had taken some tablets. He was being extremely sick, Mr Temple, in the bidet!'

'Not quite the thing,' Paul murmured.

'Absolutely, Mr Temple! People should commit suicide in their own homes. It's a very private thing –'

Paul took the manager's arm and stopped him before they entered the room. 'Suicide?' he repeated.

'That's what I said. Yes, yes, I am certain. The maid sent for me at once, and while we were waiting for the doctor I noticed a letter on the bedside table. I put it in my pocket, but as soon as Mr Lonsdale recovered he asked for the letter and tore it up. He didn't even open it.'

'Have you told Mrs Milbourne about this?'

The manager shook his head. 'It happened after she left, sir.'

'Left?' Paul frowned. 'I thought she was leaving tomorrow.'

'No, she left for Zurich this evening. Mrs Milbourne was a lady, she would never have permitted –'

Paul patted his arm and made reassuring noises. 'Leave it to me, I'll have a word with Mr Lonsdale. Don't worry.' He tapped on the door and went into Lonsdale's room as the manager departed unhappily.

Lonsdale was sitting up in bed looking pale in mauve patterned pyjamas. He glared at Paul and took a thermometer from his mouth, read his temperature and sighed.

'Has that fool of a manager sent you up here, Temple? The idiot thinks I was trying to do away with myself! As if it isn't bad enough to be ill!'

Paul sat by the bed. 'I think he's worried about the bidet.'

'It happened so suddenly,' Lonsdale looked slightly ashamed. 'I suffer from these violent migraines, Temple. Had one all day. So I took some of the tablets I keep for the purpose. I must have taken too many, that's all. It's happened before and I dare say it will happen again.'

'Fine,' said Paul. 'I'm glad it was a false alarm. Are you feeling better?'

'I'm perfectly all right.'

Paul glanced about the room. 'May I use your telephone?' He went across to the desk and picked up the receiver. 'Temple here. Can you put me through to my room, please?' He glanced at Lonsdale in the mirror. 'Steve? It's all right, darling, there's nothing to worry about. Lonsdale had a migraine and took too many tablets. I'll be down immediately.'

Paul replaced the receiver and turned to Lonsdale. 'Well, I should have a good night's sleep if I were you.' He went to the door. 'Pity you sent your sister back to London, but if you need anything in the night just give me a ring.'

'Thank you, Temple, that's very kind.'

Paul went downstairs and found Steve already in bed. She was wide awake and deeply suspicious. 'Darling,' she said as he entered the room, 'what was that ridiculous telephone call about?'

'I had to give myself an excuse to sit at Lonsdale's desk.' Paul sat on the bed beside her and took a sheet of blotting paper from his pocket. 'Can I borrow your mirror?'

He took the mirror and held it in front of the blotting paper. 'This was the top sheet on his pad,' Paul explained. 'I couldn't resist it.' The writing was spidery and legible.

Dear Margaret, it began, and then the occasional phrase could be read. . . . *deeply shocked by what you have told me . . . cannot become involved in this affair. . .* It had been a short note.

'What does he mean?' Steve asked, peering over his shoulder. 'Do you know what affair he's talking about?'

Paul shrugged and gave her back the mirror. 'It could be the Milbourne affair, I suppose.' He tossed the blotting paper into the basket.

The snow was still falling outside when Paul turned out the lights and drew the curtains. The lights of the city reflected eerily on the white roof tops. Paul opened the window very slightly and hoped Steve wouldn't notice. But she was still worrying about the note.

'Surely Lonsdale doesn't think that his sister was responsible for –' Her voice changed gear excitedly. 'Paul, you don't think Margaret Milbourne would be the person behind all this?'

He slipped down into the warm bed. 'And that she has been trying to involve her brother?'

'Yes.'

'Hence,' said Paul thoughtfully, 'the note and the suicide attempt?'

'Yes.' She wriggled close to him. 'It would be rather funny if we've been underrating Mrs Milbourne all this time.'

'It would be even funnier,' said Paul, 'if we've been underrating Mr Lonsdale.' He slipped his arm round her waist and kissed her shoulder. 'Good night, darling.'

At breakfast Lonsdale was looking his usual bluff business self. He apologised for the 'spot of bother last night' and announced that he was completely recovered. He said he was off to visit Freda Sands in hospital, but he also checked out of the hotel. He had a sensitive spot somewhere beneath the well cut suit.

Paul sipped his black coffee and watched the man climb into a car. He glanced down at his newspaper and pretended to listen while Steve planned their day. It didn't matter what they did. They were waiting, that was all, until the blackmailer made contact with Julia.

'Darling, do try to listen. This is our holiday!'

The blackmailer made contact shortly before lunchtime. Paul heard about it when he visited Vince Langham in the sickroom of the Villa Serbolini. Danny Clayton was so nervous that he brushed aside all discussion of the stitches in Vince's ribs and whether the severed muscles would heal.

'He telephoned while I was up here with the doctor,' said Danny. 'Julia took the call herself. She said it was the same man as before, the same voice. He said he was Carl Milbourne and that he wanted a final payment of a hundred and fifty thousand dollars.'

That was – yes, something like sixty thousand pounds. Roughly. Paul left: the grapes, cigarettes and back issues of *Sight & Sound* by Vince's bed, grinned encouragingly, and followed Danny from the room.

'Julia did what you told her to, she agreed to everything. I have to take the money to London and on Friday night, at eight o'clock precisely, I have to ring this number.' He showed Paul a slip of paper with the number 788 1347 jotted down.

'That's a Putney number,' said Paul.

But Putney meant nothing to Danny. 'Presumably our friend will be waiting for the call, and he'd tell me where to take the money.'

'Excellent,' said Paul cheerfully. 'Friday gives us four clear days. Just go ahead and follow my instructions, Danny.'

'Sure,' Danny said ironically. 'Just go ahead. Okay.' He put the slip of paper back in his pocket. 'I hope you know what you're doing, Paul. I'm tired of being attacked by these hoodlums.'

'You never did tell me who attacked you on the train over here,' Paul murmured.

Danny shrugged. 'I thought it was Vince Langham, because I'd seen him on the boat. But it was dark, and the more I thought about it the less certain I became. The guy who attacked me was bigger than Vince. At least I think so.'

As they came down the staircase Paul turned to look into Danny's face. 'What did you learn from Freda Sands when you visited her in hospital?'

But Danny didn't react. 'Nothing,' he said casually. 'She was convinced that Milbourne is dead. I believed her! You know, I believed that she thought so.'

Paul refused the invitation to lunch. He had to persuade Steve that their holiday was over, which might make for a busy afternoon.

'See you in London then,' said Danny.

Chapter Thirteen

Friday was a busy day. Inspector Vosper was padding about the mews house trying to ensure that he knew what was going on, and Paul was trying to ensure that the call box on Putney Heath wasn't surrounded by blue uniforms at eight o'clock when the phone call was to be made. In addition there was normal life to be led. Kate Balfour had a series of problems to be sorted out – the central heating had developed a noisy sore throat, the mended Rolls was waiting to be collected, and a Saturday appointment had been made for the lady from the posh Sunday paper. Kate believed in an orderly regimen, and blackmail cases had to be fitted into it.

Steve was ostentatiously leaving her skis at the top of the stairs and looking up train timetables to the Cairngorms.

'I don't know why the blackmailer chose a phone box on Putney Heath,' Vosper grumbled. 'It makes it difficult for my men, you know. It's a notorious meeting place for dubious characters. No decent man would go there after dark –'

'I'm sure,' Steve said icily, 'that your men will come to no harm. They can walk in pairs.'

'I meant that they could arrest everybody they saw,' Vosper explained. 'A plethora of suspects.' He grinned and turned to Paul. 'Plethora, Temple?'

Paul nodded. 'Yes, very good. But they aren't supposed to be arresting anybody!'

'Good lord no!' He went across to the desk, where Kate Balfour was speaking on the telephone. 'Any luck, detective sergeant?'

'No,' said Kate. 'He doesn't seem to be answering. They've tried his suite but there's no reply.' She hung up.

'Never mind. I have a plain clothes man tailing him. If he's playing funny games –'

When the grandfather clock at the top of the stairs struck seven Steve had her revenge. It was the final briefing session, but she burst into the operations room and announced that it was the cocktail hour.

Paul looked up from his desk in surprise. 'Cocktails?' said Charlie Vosper. Three constables stood to attention. 'If you have a can of beer in the house. . .'

'I'll fetch some from the fridge,' said Kate.

At half past seven Paul went off with Charlie Vosper to Putney Heath. They left Steve behind to wash her hair and attend to all the womanly things that had been left undone for the past ten days. It was snowing in London as well. Paul wondered why they had to go to St Moritz or the Cairngorms when the temperature at home was below freezing point.

'Of course there's one problem,' said Vosper unhappily. 'If we catch your blackmailer, what do we do with him or her? Whose case is this?'

Paul shrugged. 'I suppose the victim lives in Switzerland, but the crime was planned and executed in London. That's how we come to be out this evening.'

'As long as Walter Neider doesn't get bureaucratic about it. These Interpol characters are sticklers for procedure.'

'Leave him to me.'

Putney Heath was slightly better lit since a man had been murdered there, and police patrols tried to combat the prowling teenage gangs. But it looked a joyless place. The police car drove round the perimeter, past occasional figures huddled in overcoats, an endless line of parked cars and several courting couples until they drew up by Tibbet's Corner.

It was two minutes to eight.

The public call box was a hundred yards inside by the King's Mere. There was a street lamp glowing nearby. And on a park bench a woman police constable was being embraced by a plain clothes detective. The shabby man coming up through the subway and shuffling along the path was another policeman; he paused to forage through a litter basket.

'We'll wait here in the car,' said Vosper. 'No need to get in the way. My men know what they're doing.'

He checked on the car radio that everyone else was in position.

'Yes, sir. Mr Clayton was at the cinema this afternoon, but he came back –'

'The cinema? What does he think he's doing? Taking a bloody holiday?'

'It was an old film directed by Vince Langham, sir. At the National Film Theatre.'

'Oh.'

'But he's back at the Savoy now, waiting to make the call.'

'Right.' Vosper glanced at his watch. It was eight o'clock. 'Here we go.'

They sat in the car while Danny Clayton made his phone call, a policeman recorded the conversation, and the courting couple watched to see who answered the telephone. When the man left the call box the shabby man turned away from the litter basket and followed him.

At five past eight Paul saw the man leave the heath and go off towards the railway station. He was a stoutly built man with a limp, about thirty-five but slow in his movements.

'There goes the messenger,' said Charlie Vosper. 'Now for the real villain.'

Inspector Vosper flicked the switch on his car radio. 'Get me Gabriel,' he said biblically. 'Gabriel? This is Beelzebub. What are the arrangements?'

'The hand-over is at the Fancy Free Club in Soho, sir, any time after eleven o'clock. That's a place run by Tully –'

'I know all about Tully's fun palace,' Vosper snapped. 'Move on to phase two of the operation, Gabriel. Get moving.' He turned to Paul. 'The Fancy Free is a high class strip joint, you pay more and get less –'

Paul nodded. 'Tully is a friend of mine.'

The inspector looked surprised.

'I'd better let Steve know we're going there,' Paul continued meekly. 'She has her doubts about Tully.'

When Paul and Steve arrived at the Fancy Free they were shown straight through the side door and up to Tully's office. They were whisked through so quickly that Steve didn't have a chance to examine the photographs in the foyer or to wonder what a *'sexorama'* could possibly be.

She seemed quite interested in the girls going to and from their dressing-rooms disguised as Siamese cats and she asked innocently what the men did in the show. But they were soon in the owner's luxury apartment.

'Steve, girl, you're looking gorgeous!' Tully embraced her as an old friend. 'So this is what the women who wear clothes are wearing these days?' He slapped her on the bottom and then turned to shake hands with Paul. 'Great to see you again, Paul. I hear I'm supposed to be on the side of the law tonight?'

'I'm afraid so –'

'It'll scare the life out of my boys.' He roared with laughter. 'If only coppers didn't look so much like bloody coppers! I'll have to tell everybody they're here to check up on Dolly Brazier's attack.'

'How is Dolly?' asked Steve.

'Oh, she's making the most of the drama,' Tully said with a laugh. 'She came back to work yesterday, looking none the worse but talking as if she's the heroine in a gangster film.' He pressed a button on the intercom. 'Send up Dolly Brazier,' he ordered.

'Okay, boss,' said a blurred voice at the other end. 'By the way, we've got the fuzz in the cloakroom. The girls have switched to the Vicarage Tea Party until we get rid of –'

'That's all right, Cyril. Show them up here.'

There was a pause at the other end. 'Whatever you say, boss.'

Tully opened up his cocktail cabinet and distributed large brandies while Inspector Vosper and two plain clothes policemen came into the room and sat uncomfortably on a sofa. One of the policemen nursed a tape recorder on his lap.

'Perhaps,' Steve said to break the atmosphere, 'I could go downstairs and have a chat with Dolly –'

'No. I'd rather you didn't,' said Vosper. 'I'd like you to hear this tape record, Mrs Temple.'

'Go ahead,' said Tully, 'make yourselves at home. There's a plug beside the bookcase.'

Tully helped the constable plug it in and set the tape's position. Then they sat back and listened to the telephone call in comfort, sipping brandy and smoking Fancy Free cigars. They could hear the ringing sound, and then it stopped.

'Is that 788 1347?' asked Danny Clayton's voice.

'Have you got the money?'

'Yes,' said Danny. 'Now what do you want me to do?'

'Listen,' said the man, 'and listen carefully. Put the money in a case and take it to the Fancy Free Club in Soho –'

'Now?' Danny sounded surprised. 'Tonight?'

'Yeah, tonight. Any time after eleven. Leave the case with the cloakroom attendant. Give the girl a pound and tell her someone called Lesley will pick it up later.'

Danny was being slow to understand in order to get as much of the man's voice on tape as possible. 'Someone called Lesley?' he repeated.

'That's right. Fancy Free Club, Old Compton Street, after eleven o'clock. Have you got that?'

'Yes, I've got it.'

'Okay, that's all, Mr Clayton. Good night.'

The policeman switched off the tape recorder.

'I know that voice,' Steve said excitedly. 'It's the man who brought the car – you remember, Paul, he said his name was Stone and that you'd told him to bring the car –'

'That's right, Mrs Temple,' said Inspector Vosper. 'When he left the box we had him tailed to Notting Hill Gate. He has a flat out there.'

'You didn't pick him up, did you?' asked Paul.

'We're not that stupid, Temple. It isn't Stone we're after. We want this character called Lesley.'

Paul grunted. 'Lesley! That's just a cover name for –'

'Hey!' Tully had risen to his feet in bewilderment. 'I thought Mickey Stone was out of circulation?'

Vosper began to explain that he had walked with a limp and was looking rather fragile, but then he understood. 'Oh, I see. But it was Stone who did over Dolly Brazier, was it? No wonder he limps. But he's a tough character. A stretch in prison is the only thing –'

The moral homily was interrupted by a bleep from the inspector's inside pocket. He took out a short wave radio transmitter. 'Excuse me,' he muttered. 'Yes?'

'Eleven o'clock, sir. Mr Clayton is just entering the club.'

Tully went to the window and peered down into the street. He grinned and pointed out to Paul the three parked cars and the two loiterers who were keeping the premises under observation. There was no fooling an old hand at the game.

'Clever,' said Paul. 'But our blackmailer is not a professional like you, Tully. This is an amateur.'

'Even so,' said Tully, 'I think it would be better if the inspector and his two yes-men stayed up here. You and I can go downstairs and wait for the collection. My boys will handle any trouble.'

Vosper was doubtful, but Paul agreed before the police could object. It was sound thinking.

'And don't bother to search the office,' Tully said cynically. 'I knew you were coming, so it's clean.'

The three policemen laughed heartily at the joke.

'I'll come down as well,' said Steve. 'I've always wondered what these clubs were like, and Paul refuses to take me. I think I might even enjoy it.'

'It's all right,' Tully boomed, 'they're doing the Vicarage Tea Party! Nothing that a husband wouldn't want his wife to see.'

The club was filled with people and smoke and noise; there were tables where men ate expensive meals in the half light; at the rear of the floor was a bar where more men stood drinking alone. The décor was red plush with gilt trimmings, which seemed appropriate. Up on stage two young ladies were stripping before an apoplectic vicar, while a clarinet and guitar maintained the erotic mood.

'Isn't this rather dull?' Steve enquired as the girls got down to their underwear. 'The men in the audience aren't even sweating.'

'They bring on the toasted tea cakes next,' said Tully, 'that's when the real fun starts.'

Dolly Brazier was out in the cloakroom, dressed in provocative furs and fishnet. The effect of her naked midriff was slightly spoiled by a large band of sticking plaster. She looked as always like the cheerful housemaid who arranges flowers when the first act curtain goes up. She was waving vigorously at Paul when Danny Clayton arrived with his weekend case.

'Good evening, sir,' said Dolly.

'Hi. I want to leave this case with you. Someone called Lesley will pick it up later this evening.'

'A gentleman?' asked Dolly.

Danny looked confused. 'Well – I suppose so.' He slapped a pound note on the counter. 'Here, this is for your trouble.'

'Thanks very much,' said Dolly. 'I'll see that Lesley gets the case whether she's male or he's female.' She giggled as Danny came through into the club.

'We'd better wait over here,' Tully said to Paul. 'We can see everything that's going on, except that they can't see us. This is where the bouncers keep an eye on the customers.'

It was a dark recess beside the steps which had been a prompt box in more sophisticated days, when exquisite little revues had kept the customers amused. Paul and Steve sat in comfortable armchairs and watched the dancers waiting in the wings with their bird-like feathers.

'Darling,' said Steve suddenly, 'look who's over there at the bar!'

Danny had walked across to the bar to fetch a drink and he was standing by a dishevelled man in a flying jacket. Of the two Danny was looking the more embarrassed, as if he didn't want Vince Langham to think he habitually visited strip clubs.

'He's a film director,' Tully explained.

'What's he doing here?'

Tully laughed happily. 'He wants to use the Fancy Free in a new film that he's making. It's about a girl who starts in a place like this, makes a few useful contacts and goes on the stage, then ends up as an alcoholic in Hollywood. Sounds a lot of old malarkey to me – my girls end up getting married and having five kids. But Vince Langham is a romantic, and a film like that will be good for my business.'

'I'd have thought,' Paul said reflectively, 'that he'd have used one of the clubs in New York.'

'They're all the same. London, New York, Hamburg. We had the television people here a few months ago, pretending this was Berlin in the nineteen-twenties.'

The conversation came to an end with Danny drinking a rapid whisky and leaving the club. It was all according to plan, but Vince obviously thought he had been brushed off again. He glared after the retreating Danny and then went to sit with a delectable blonde stripper.

'Is he here for the money or the girl?' asked Steve.

'We'd have to watch and see.'

They didn't have to watch for long. The blackmailer had obviously been waiting outside for Danny to leave and was now coming down the stairs. He paused and went across to the cloakroom.

'That's him!' said Paul. 'Wait here, Steve.'

Paul slipped out of the prompt box and hurried through the darkened auditorium. He reached the cloakroom a moment after Dolly had handed over the weekend case. She called out a gleeful, 'Hello, darling, I was waving at you!' as he ran past.

'Wait a minute, Lonsdale!' called Paul. 'I think you should stay for a few explanations.'

Lonsdale spun round with the case in his hands. 'Temple!' He glanced back up the stairs and into the club. 'What are you doing here?' But the converging policemen and Tully with his bouncers gave the answer.

'I thought you were in Switzerland,' said Lonsdale. 'I telephoned your hotel this morning –'

Paul smiled. 'Actually you didn't speak to the manager, you spoke to a man called Neider. We thought you'd probably check up on me. Hand over that case!'

Lonsdale had waited until the two policemen on the stairs had reached him. He grabbed them both by their tunics and pulled them down on to Paul. Then he ran.

A chorus of police whistles began to blow. When Paul reached the top of the stairs he found a flurry of bodies as the bouncers fought their way through a panic-stricken swarm of customers who thought it was a police raid. Police cars arrived with screeching brakes as Lonsdale broke free. He swung the weekend case at Charlie Vosper, slammed a car door on its driver and darted into the road.

'Look out!' shouted Paul. He reached for Lonsdale's hand, but it was too late. A police car with klaxon wailing had hit Lonsdale and skidded over his body.

The confusion on the pavement increased, people were shouting and a woman began to cry hysterically. The crowd pressed round to watch the blood gushing from under the car.

'He ran straight into us,' said the driver helplessly. 'We were coming to lend assistance –'

'I know, I know,' said Vosper.

Paul knelt down by the twisted body; Lonsdale was dead with the weekend case still clasped to his chest. He took the case and handed it to Vosper. 'Don't bother to open it,' he murmured. 'Half a dozen books, that's all it contains.'

Somebody behind them said that an ambulance was on its way. Paul shrugged and went off in search of Steve. There was little that an ambulance could do except clear up the mess. Paul found her at the back of the crowd consoling Dolly Brazier.

'Poor Lonsdale,' she said to Paul with a shudder. 'I didn't like him, but –'

Paul led the two women into the club. 'I suppose it's poetic; the affair started with a road accident in Geneva, and ends with one in Soho. We need some of Tully's brandy.'

'Just a moment, Miss Brazier!' It was Inspector Vosper at his most official. 'I must ask you to accompany me to New Scotland Yard. There are one or two questions. . .'

Paul looked quickly at Dolly. She was crying and her make-up had run to reveal two scars on her face. Of course – Paul cursed himself for being so susceptible to blondes. Dolly had known Maurice Lonsdale!

'She needs a drink,' said Paul. 'Come back upstairs and ask your questions in comfort.'

Actually it was the blood and the sudden violence that had reduced Dolly to tears, it had shocked her. 'I hated him,' she said mildly after the large brandy. 'I lived with him for a few weeks, because he was a millionaire and he said he would help me with my career. But he always frightened me.'

Vosper muttered something about feather-headed showgirls.

'I wasn't even that when I met Mr Lonsdale. I was a typist with the Freda Sands Agency, and I soon got the sack from there.' She began sobbing again. 'I'm no good at anything except looking decorative. And now with these scars –'

Paul put an arm round her shoulders. 'It's all right, Dolly, don't upset yourself. You simply have a talent for making the wrong friends, but we'd look after you.' He smiled. 'After all, you did warn me, didn't you?'

'I heard Mr Lonsdale arranging to have you taken care of. He knew I was going to warn you and he didn't seem to mind. But then Mickey Stone . . . It was terrible. I'm glad he's dead!'

Inspector Vosper stood over her and looked severe. 'There's only one other question, Miss Brazier. Did you know what was in the weekend case when it was brought in this evening?'

Dolly shook her head and looked dizzily innocent. 'It wasn't until Mr Lonsdale came in and told me his name was Lesley that I realised I was involved in trouble again. I would have told Paul, but then you all appeared and the whistles started blowing. . .'

Paul sighed and poured himself another brandy. She might be telling the truth, more or less, or she might have hoped that Lonsdale would turn out to be sweet and generous. Poor Dolly was never very clever at knowing the truth for herself. But she wasn't a criminal.

'Feather-headed showgirls,' muttered Vosper.

Chapter Fourteen

She was a terrifying girl who chain-smoked miniature cigars and coughed continuously into her tape recorder. She peered at him through a mass of tangled hair and asked a question which included the phrases *comme il faut* and *fortior quam prudentior erat* and concluded with something about *Weltanschauung*.

'I beg your pardon?' asked Paul.

'Whither the novel?' she asked, brushing ash off her ancient miniskirt.

'I leave questions like that to Scott Reed,' said Paul. 'He lies awake at night worrying in case the novel is dead.' The girl was looking bewildered. 'Scott Reed is my publisher.'

'I know.' She sighed, and launched into a theory about nonfiction art which derived from Truman Capote and the dignity of the *'Fact'*. 'Have you no ambitions to create in this new form?'

'No.' Paul glanced at his watch. The girl had been given an hour and a half by Kate Balfour. Only an hour and a quarter to go. 'Would you like a drink?'

'Beer, please, Mr Temple.'

Paul called down the stairs for Kate to bring up a can from the fridge. Whatever happened to those old-fashioned journalists who ask about the money you earn and whether your wife is jealous of the heroines you invent? He poured himself a whisky.

'Of course F.R. Leavis would question the whole moral basis –'

They were interrupted by an approaching commotion; Kate Balfour was saying, 'No no, you'll have to wait, he's being interviewed for one of the colour comics,' and somebody else was being unimpressed. Thank God. Paul knew how they'd felt at the relief of Mafeking. Relieved.

'Don't worry, darling, I'm terribly good with reporters.'

That sounded like the clipped self-confident voice of Margaret Milbourne.

'Yeah, well, I mean, I've got something to tell the press, haven't I?' The Bronx accents of Danny Clayton.

The girl switched off her tape recorder as the door burst open and Danny came in with a can of beer in each hand. He was followed by Margaret Milbourne and a protesting Kate. Luckily the girl had written articles called 'Whither Theatre?' for *Isis* so she was impressed with Margaret.

'Will you drink it out of the can?' asked Danny. 'Or shall I find you a glass?'

'Perhaps I should come back some other time?' she said.

'No,' said Steve as she joined him, 'it's usually like this. Yesterday we had policemen all over the house. I'm afraid we've had a busy time with this blackmail affair.'

'Thank God it's over,' said Margaret. 'The whole business has been a nightmare. Even now it just doesn't make sense.' She sat tragically in the egg-shaped chair facing Paul's desk. 'How on earth did it all happen, Mr Temple?'

Paul waited while Steve poured drinks for everyone.

'It started when Vince Langham heard about the fire in Santa Barbara. He was directing Julia in a film at the time, and some years later he decided to write a book about it. Thanks very much. When the book was finished Vince sent it to Freda Sands to be typed, and the woman who typed it was Dolly Brazier. She had a very temporary job with the Sands Agency at the time.'

'Ah,' said Steve, 'I wondered how Dolly came into it.'

'Vince showed the book to Carl Milbourne, who bought it outright and persuaded Vince to use a pseudonym – Richard Randolph.'

'That's clear enough,' said Margaret impatiently. 'But how did my brother become involved?'

'Maurice Lonsdale had lent your husband a large sum of money and he wanted immediate repayment. They were discussing this when Carl mentioned the book *Too Young to Die*. Well, Lonsdale was already operating several rackets and he realised that Julia Carrington was an extremely wealthy woman. He decided that the book could be used as a means of blackmail.'

Danny Clayton sat on the floor and muttered, 'Too bloody right.'

'Carl Milbourne went to Geneva because Lonsdale told him to. He went and saw Julia, and they did a deal together, but on the way home he was knocked down and killed. Yes, he was dead, but Lonsdale was determined that the plan should still go ahead. So Lonsdale telephoned Julia saying that he was Carl, saying that the accident had been a fake. And later,' Paul said turning to Margaret Milbourne, 'he put a doubt into your mind about the accident.'

'That was when he sent me the hat?'

Paul nodded. 'The note was in your husband's handwriting, but it was an undated note which Carl had previously sent to your brother. Lonsdale simply added the date.'

'Okay,' said Danny, 'but what was the point? Why should Lonsdale want to convince Mrs Milbourne that her husband was still alive?'

'It was Julia he wanted to convince,' said Paul. 'But he knew that if Margaret Milbourne thought her husband was alive she'd say so in a loud voice, and that way Julia would hear about it.' Paul smiled complacently. 'What Lonsdale didn't bargain for was the fact that Margaret would consult me. He was nervous about me; he even hired that man Stone to scare me off and to beat up Dolly Brazier.'

Paul went and poured himself another drink, and while he was passing made sure that the girl hadn't got the tape recorder switched on. She hadn't. She was a feature writer.

'I'm afraid your brother was a pretty ruthless character, Mrs Milbourne. He beat up Dolly to show he meant business and he attacked Danny in the train to Switzerland. I think he even scared you, didn't he? He frightened you into telling that story about Danny asking for money?'

She nodded. 'But I didn't know anyone would be killed. That poor man on the houseboat –'

'– was meant to be me,' Paul intervened. 'When did you first realise your brother had been lying to you?'

'When I reached St Moritz. The night we arrived in St Moritz my brother came to my room. He was angry and he'd been drinking. He said the most awful things, about Carl and that wretched Freda Sands. He said that Carl had been blackmailing Julia Carrington and that the blackmailing had to continue.' She was near to tears now, but she managed to smile. 'I'm glad Freda Sands broke her leg. I wish it had been her neck! Carl would never have been unfaithful to me if she hadn't encouraged him.'

Paul sighed with relief. He had been worried about telling Margaret where Freda Sands fitted into the case. 'You were talking about Lonsdale,' he murmured, 'the night he came to your room.'

'Maurice said that if I didn't help he would throw suspicion on to me. He was horrible, just like he used to be when we were children together.'

'Well, he did throw suspicion on to you,' said Steve, 'the moment you left St Moritz.'

Margaret looked up in surprise. 'He did?'

'He pretended to commit suicide and leave a note behind, blaming you for everything.'

Margaret began crying quietly to herself.

'It was all made more complicated,' Paul continued, 'because Vince Langham was blundering about, getting in the way generally and trying a spot of blackmail himself. He wanted Julia to make another film with him and he didn't mind using the book as moral persuasion. If Julia had said yes I imagine Vince would have sued the publishers and done his damnedest to get the book back.'

'My brother,' Margaret said between tears, 'was worried about Vince Langham. He said he was going to do something . . .'

'He did. First of all he dropped Vince's cigarette case in the snow, and then he attacked him with a knife. I doubt whether Vince will ever risk writing a book again.'

Steve smiled and asked what would happen now to *Too Young to Die*. Would it be up to Wallace and Sainsbury to decide –?

'It doesn't matter any more,' Danny Clayton interrupted. 'I telephoned Julia this morning and told her everything that has happened. She's decided to tell the truth about herself, about Hollywood and the fire and everything.'

Paul was surprised. 'You mean she really is going to write her autobiography?'

'No.' Danny laughed. 'Julia can't even write a letter to her stockbroker. No, she's been negotiating with *World Magazine* in New York, and they want *you* to write the story of Julia Carrington.'

'Me?' Paul laughed apologetically. 'No no, that's quite impossible. I'm a novelist, and besides –' He caught the girl with the tape recorder looking suddenly respectful. 'No, I'm sorry. I don't really approve of facts. I leave those things to Charlie Vosper.'

The tape recorder was running again, and downstairs the telephone began to ring.

'Would this mean,' Steve asked Danny Clayton, 'that we would have to return to St Moritz?'

Danny nodded. 'I'm afraid it would. But you can stay with us, and Julia isn't as bad to live with as –'

'He'll write it!'

Paul was about to argue when Kate Balfour poked her head round the door. 'It's *World Magazine* on the telephone, Mr Temple.'

'I refuse to speak to them!'

'But they're ringing from New York –'

'Leave it to me,' said Steve. 'Don't worry, darling, Danny and I will look after everything. You carry on with your quality interview.'

Paul turned in despair to the girl. 'All right, you were asking me about Dr Leavis. . .'